A Horse for Christmas Morning
and Other Stories

THE DERRYDALE PRESS

FOXHUNTERS' LIBRARY

A HORSE FOR CHRISTMAS MORNING

and Other Stories

GORDON GRAND

With a new introduction by Henry Hooker, M.F.H.

THE DERRYDALE PRESS
Lanham and New York

THE DERRYDALE PRESS

Published in the United States of America
by The Derrydale Press
4720 Boston Way, Lanham, Maryland 20706

Distributed by NATIONAL BOOK NETWORK, INC.

Copyright 1939, 1943, 1945, 1948 by Gordon Grand
Copyright © 1970 by Olin Corporation
First Derrydale Printing 2001

Library of Congress Control Number: 2001093622
ISBN 1-58667-074-3 (cloth : alk paper)

♾™ The paper used in this publication meets the minimum requirements of
American National Standard for Information Sciences—Permanence of
Paper for Printed Library Materials, ANSI/NISO Z39.48–1992.
Manufactured in the United States of America.

TABLE OF CONTENTS

Foreword vii

Introduction xi

A Horse for Christmas Morning 3

Mr. Nip and Mr. Tuck 49

Faith, Perfect Faith 63

Mr. Henry P. Throckmorton 83

FOREWORD

These four little sporting tales are unique. For this reason something of their background and of the author will perhaps add to your understanding and enjoyment of them.

During his lifetime my father gained a reputation as one of the foremost writers of American sporting fiction, particularly stories of horses, riding and fox hunting. Frankly, this recognition was a surprise to him for he was not a professional writer. He was a lawyer and businessman and wrote simply for the pleasure it gave him and the enjoyment his stories gave to others. But he wrote of a world he knew intimately from boyhood and enjoyed so much.

His series of five books of short stories began with "The Silver Horn" published in 1932 and ended with "The Southborough Fox" in 1939. They were published in limited editions only and have been out of print for many years. The last popular edition of a collection of his stories (*The Millbeck Hounds*) was published by Charles Scribner's Sons in 1947. Over the years, and continuing today, his stories have appeared in anthologies of sporting literature—and in anthologies of American humor, too. They can be found along with such entertaining pieces as "Lost" with the memorable Mr. Jorrocks by R. S. Surtees; "Philippa's Fox Hunt," by Somerville and Ross; "The First Day," from Sassoon's *Memoirs of a Fox Hunting Man*; "The Man Who Hunts and Never Jumps," by Anthony Trollope; "Squire Weston in Pursuit" from Fielding's *Tom Jones*, and others.

The four stories in this book were written by Father in the decade of the 40's—one every two years or so apart—and were never published; nor did he intend them to be published. They were privately printed in editions of less than 100 each and sent by him as Christmas books to the new generation of "young entry" riders and fox hunters among his close friends and neighbors. Each grandchild always received a copy with the gentle suggestion to the parent that the story be read aloud, which Father did for us when we were growing up.

Father was also a constant and generous letter writer to his family. It was natural, therefore, in "A Horse for Christmas Morning" that he used an exchange of letters to unfold his story.

Colonel Weatherford, Arthur Pendleton (the Colonel's neighbor), young John Weatherford (the Colonel's nephew), Judge Culpepper of Virginia, and Eddie Walsh (expert horseman and Colonel Weatherford's flamboyant groom), all of whom appear in these stories, were the characters in many of his published works. They were composites of people we know, particularly Colonel Weatherford and Eddie Walsh. The setting was Millbrook, New York, where we as a family lived and hunted for many years.

Father's contribution to the sporting world, particularly riding and fox hunting, was not only to its literature but to the development and encouragement of the sport as well. His stories had this purpose, too. He reminded us that those who are privileged to participate have an obligation to devote time and effort to preserve the sport for others to enjoy. For this reason, when family and business affairs permitted, he gave generously of his time and effort. He—and mother, too, for she was a bold and expert horsewoman—during their lifetime judged many horse shows, including the National Horse Show at Madison Square Garden.

If these tales bring enjoyment, and hopefully a little laughter, they will have served their purpose well. Perhaps they will encourage a "young entry" of today to be "way forrard with hounds—a day's furrow forrard," as I know they did some years ago.

My sister, Mrs. Edwin Thorne, who also gave her permission to have these stories published, joins me in the foreword. The line between sentiment and sentimentality is thin at best, and this is particularly true for both of us in connection with these stories which bring back so many happy memories.

Gordon Grand, Jr.

INTRODUCTION

When I began foxhunting in the 1950s, Billy Haggard introduced me to sporting art and literature. He even gave me *A Horse for Christmas Morning* and *Faith, Perfect Faith*, two Christmas stories Gordon Grand had written and privately published in editions of only one hundred copies for the children of his hunt. Having already read Gordon Grand's series of Colonel Weatherford books with great pleasure, I was excited to obtain the lesser known children's Christmas stories. I regarded Gordon Grand then, as I do now, as the leading American author of foxhunting fiction. He had the literary skills to make his stories simultaneously amusing and meaningful. His characters spoke in their appropriate idiom and demonstrated their appropriate values. Gordon Grand's descriptions had an economy of words because of the inevitability of the exactly right next word used in his narratives. I read the two stories Haggard gave me. They were charming. My children loved them. I made copies and sent them to the children in our hunt for their parents to read to them. It was a great success.

Although I searched for copies of the other two stories and put in standing orders for them at the sporting booksellers, I never had any success in my quest to locate them. Then I heard that Gordon Grand, Jr., was Chairman of Olin Corporation. I wrote him a letter and inquired if he might know where I could locate the two missing stories. To my surprise and delight, he called me very shortly thereafter to discuss my interest in his father's writing. He was very proud of his father's accomplishments. As the conversation went on, he began to muse about his own career. He obviously had a signal success in business, but he seemed more impressed by the lessons and the lifestyle contained in his father's books and stories. Gordon Grand, Jr. cut to the chase and talked to me about what really mattered to him. He seemed to indicate that his father had lived a more entertaining life than he and wondered, as well, whether his father had left a more worthwhile legacy.

Then he changed course and told me that he had been prompted by my letter to go rummaging in his attic. He had found an original of each of the two Christmas stories that I was missing and was sending them to me as he knew his father would have been pleased for me to have them. A few days later, the stories arrived with this letter of transmission:

Dear Mr. Hooker,

I am happy to say that I have found two of father's Christmas stories, which I do not believe you have read. It is a pleasure for me to send them to you for your personal library and I do hope you enjoy reading them. I know that father would be very pleased to have these stories in such appreciative hands. Perhaps our ways will some day cross and should you come to New York and have a minute do give me a ring.

Sincerely,

Gordon Grand

I was touched that a man so busy and with such responsibilities would spend his time looking in his attic for something for a stranger. I wrote to thank him:

Dear Mr. Grand:

> *Mr. Nip and Mr. Tuck* and *Henry P. Throckmorton* arrived to-
> day in excellent condition. As I did last year with *A Horse for
> Christmas Morning*, I plan to send a copy of one of the stories
> to each member of the Hillsboro Hounds. Judging from last
> year's response, it will be a great success although I can't say
> who enjoys them the most—the adults or the children.
>
> When I wrote you about the possibility of borrowing a
> copy of your father's Christmas stories, I never dreamed
> that I would be able to obtain the originals of the two that
> I lacked. I certainly appreciate your taking the time and
> trouble to locate them for me, and thank you very much for
> making my "Gordon Grand Christmas Story Collection"
> complete. You could not have given me anything of greater
> value. Although I had wanted so long to read them, I found
> them to be even more delicious than the anticipation.
>
> If it is convenient for you, I would like to come and
> thank you personally when next I am in New York. In the
> interim, I hope that all the pleasure of the children of our
> hunt, who will now have the opportunity to enjoy your
> father's wisdom and humor, will bring you some satis-
> faction for your generosity.
>
> Sincerely,
>
> Henry W. Hooker

Not long after, I saw that the Winchester Press, a subsidiary
of the Olin Corporation with the Olympic horseman Bill
Steinkraus as its editor, was publishing a limited edition of
A Horse For Christmas Morning, containing all four stories,
with a foreword by Gordon Grand, Jr. himself. His foreword was a thoughtful elaboration on the subjects he had
raised in our discussion. I obtained a few copies, which I
have since enjoyed giving or lending to friends.

This was not the end of the affair. The following spring my wife, Alice, procured a pair of Easter chicks for our children. The chicks were duly fussed over, progressed to the barn, and placed under the protection of the grooms. All went well. The chicks grew into White Leghorn roosters. One was named Mr. Throckmorton in commemoration of one of the children's favorite stories written by Gordon Grand. Then, at the beginning of the hunt season, Alice went to the barn to have a look around, a euphemism for an inspection. The roosters attacked her from the rear, flying up to spur her on her calves and so on. It was a simple territorial dispute but the sentinel roosters were banished to Bill and Joyce Brown's Fox Camp in Mississippi. No amount of entreaty could change the decree. Horses, hounds, and roosters were loaded in the van and headed for Mississippi with us to follow. The children were excited not only to be going foxhunting at a favorite place, but also to be taking the roosters to their new home with Joyce Brown, the queen of all pet protectors.

However, when we arrived at Fox Camp the van, the horses, the pack of hounds, and the roosters were missing. We immediately divided into search parties and soon located our wrecked van. The groom had missed a turn in the rain and rolled the van off an embankment onto its side in a soybean field. When we found them, horses that had been upside down were liberated, hounds had escaped and gone hunting, the groom had gone to jail, and only one rooster, Mr. Throckmorton, remained. He was perched upon the high side, covered with manure, missing all but one of his tail feathers, and observing the rescue party with skeptical eyes. The horses were salvaged and sent to camp with their feathered traveling companion while I blew for hounds and waited for them to sift back to their unusual casting ground.

When I got back to camp, Joyce had washed Mr. Throckmorton, but his one tail feather was still greenish. When I
remarked on this condition, I was informed that he was no
longer Mr. Throckmorton. Bill had changed his name to
Disaster in commemoration of the great Mississippi van
wreck. Poor old Disaster had lost his confidence along with
his plumage. He would not even cluck, much less crow. Bill
promised to make a shelf for Disaster outside the window
by their bed so Joyce would know Disaster felt safe. In due
course, we got our van driver out of jail and limped back to
Nashville with the bent up van, the children, and the
horses. The hounds and Disaster stayed in Mississippi.

As soon as we got everything patched up, we took the
children and some of their friends back to Fox Camp. When
we got there, I realized something was wrong but did not
know what. It was Disaster. That rooster was missing. Bill
explained everything. He said that he was feeding Disaster
on his shelf by the window and Disaster's tail feathers
started growing back. As soon as they did, he started clucking and crowing again. Bill moved him out to the stables
where he would not wake Bill and Joyce up. This did not
work because Disaster's tail feathers continued to grow
and his crowing got louder. So Bill moved him down by the
lake to a little chicken house across the pasture.

Disaster was clucking and promenading. His new ac-
commodations with the hens suited him fine. Then one of
the children introduced the question, "If Disaster is crowing and strutting with the lady chickens and making
speeches by his clucking, why isn't he Mr. Throckmorton
again?" This was certainly a serious and perplexing question. We took a whole day at camp to discuss it. Finally, a
vote was taken that night at dinner, and Mr. Throckmorton
was restored his rightful name. The crowing sounds the
next morning were muted enough by the distance to the

lake so that Bill said he could have slept through them if he had not already been awake tacking the horses to go hunting at dawn.

As the first fiery streaks kindled the eastern sky, we drew hounds out of the kennel to the accompaniment of the most heraldic cock-a-doodle-doing ever heard in those parts. When, after a wonderful morning of galloping to hounds on loamy soil, we returned to camp, Mr. Throckmorton was clucking something fierce. Bill pointed over the pasture. A red tail hawk was gliding around in the sky. "Uh oh," Bill said, watching the hawk land on a rock that stuck about two feet out of the pasture. Mr. Throckmorton charged that hawk and gave it a double-cluck piece of his mind about landing that close to the hens. It seemed that the hawk heard him because it retreated to the safety of the sky and began making slow circles above the pasture. Mr. Throckmorton, the defender, clucked great satisfaction with his work and turned back, strutting towards his admiring audience at the hen house.

However, with terrifying swiftness and incredible accuracy, the hawk folded its wings and stooped in a dive like a bullet directly at Mr. Throckmorton, who was struck, stunned, and clutched in the red tail's powerful talons. Poor Mr. Throckmorton was all higgle-dee piggle-dee as the hawk dragged him to that protruding rock and cast off with its protesting burden. Indeed, at the moment it became airborne, the hawk seemed to sink back towards the ground and we thought for an instant that it might drop its quarry long enough for us to effect a rescue operation. But, with a powerful pump of its wings, the red tail ascended into the sky, its prize firmly in its grasp. Higher and higher, it rose, circled, and set its course. Mr. Throckmorton's squawking faded out of earshot as he was transported southwest toward the delta country. I do not know whether he crossed the big river, but I can report that I watched him until that speck disappeared from view, and I sorrowed for that plucky rooster.

I turned to the children. They were busy with their own concerns, some wiping away a tear, others composing an expression of stoicism on their faces. Then, one of them said in a proud voice, "Did you see that rooster take on that hawk? That must be the bravest rooster there has ever been. You may be lunch, Mr. Throckmorton, but you sure told that hawk a thing or two." Suddenly in agreement, they all stood in their stirrups and began waiving their bats in salute. "Goodbye, Mr. Throckmorton. Goodbye," they called to him. I looked at those children, their faces trans-fixed on the sky, calling farewell and paying tribute to a friend honorably vanquished protecting his home and harem.

I thought: "I have read some great sporting writers. Some of them could write dialogue, and some could write dialect. A few might even write dog dialogue. But Gordon Grand has to be the only sporting writer I ever read who could teach these children to speak rooster and to appreci-ate the nobility of his message."

Henry Hooker, M.F.H.
Hunting Hollow
Nashville, Tennessee

A Horse for
Christmas Morning

A HORSE FOR
CHRISTMAS MORNING

Cavendish Culpepper
to
John Weatherford II

Dear Young friend:
My compliments and good wishes. I pray that your affairs,
your health and your studies all prosper.
This letter is for the purpose of ascertaining whether it
would give you pleasure to visit me again during the ap-
proaching Christmas vacation. If so, and you will so write
me, the matter will be laid before your uncle, Colonel
Weatherford. I have every confidence that you will express
your feelings freely. It is conceivable that you may have
many high plans for the holiday season, more appealing to
youth than engaging in sport with so ancient a group of
gentlemen as your La Marquisville friends. This we will
readily understand.
Your same little horse will be available. Uncle Up, Slim,
Double Slim, your personal boy Updown, Sarah, Old Bess
and my other retainers will be at your disposal. The cus-
tomary assortment of exhilarating, unbroken colts are on
hand for your servant Walsh to ride.

Today week, being the occasion of your friend the Sheriff's birthday, his many neighbors did me the honor of foregathering here at Cavendish House to notice the event. They continued their felicitations through the night and paid their civilities by remaining for breakfast, an additional pleasure to me.

During the afternoon of the dinner I bethought me of the life-buoy I had purchased close to fifty years ago from the ferry-boat captain to throw out to the Sheriff. It was the day he jumped his horse into the Potomac River, thinking it to be Skelly's Creek here at Marquisville. I dispatched Uncle Up to find it. With Mrs. Padget's assistance we made a circular floral decoration of the life-buoy for the center of the table. After some preliminary and forceful protestations, in no sense lending themselves to recording, the Sheriff took our display in good part. He remarked that he would indeed give much could he again address his horse to so formidable an obstacle as the Potomac River in so light and confident a manner.

This occasioned the company to reminisce upon the happy events and good sport of other days. Your stay among us was mentioned and the wish freely expressed that we might anticipate the pleasure of another visit.

The Sheriff, making a great clatter among the dishes, said to Major Padget, Mr. Stringfellow, Gen. Olcott, Mr. Churchill, Mr. Randolph, Dr. Prentice and the others, "Gentlemen, I am very fond of that brat of a boy. Uncle Up, you worthless black rascal, my glass, my glass."

I make bold to quote the Sheriff's own words, feeling that his manner of speech would the better recall us all to your memory.

My dear John, you would indeed afford pleasure to a group of stalwart old country gentlemen by hunting, shooting and making merry with them, at this season of the year.

Might I presume to suggest that the Yuletide spirit is of the same pattern the world over. You will find it in our quiet, remote valley of Virginia, in your native Boston and in the Merry England of Mr. Dickens.

Among those who stayed on for breakfast was your friend Mr. Jimmie Clarke, the shooting-dog trainer and newspaper reporter. He seems to not have quite comprehended our conversation but rather to have gathered that you were definitely coming to me. As a result, the La Marquisville paper printed the following article.

The leading gentlemen of this place are anticipating a visit from Master John Weatherford II, the nephew of that famous Master of Hounds and breeder of thoroughbreds, Colonel John Fortescue Weatherford of Millbeck, New York.

John Weatherford II stayed with Judge Culpepper a year ago and is fondly remembered by the hunting and shooting fraternity. Though but a small boy, he rode well forward. No fence was too formidable, no day too long for him. His body servant, Colonel Weatherford's groom, E. Walsh, proved himself a competent dog handler through winning the La Marquisville-Harroldsburg ratcatching match with Master John's terrier Hiccup, and was singularly successful along certain other lines which brought him in conflict with the law. Walsh was a likable fellow and a fine horseman. We hope he will be again in attendance upon his young master.

I was in the village this morning and as a result of Mr. Clarke's article, Mr. Peckett at the bank, Mr. Moody in the hardware store, the young lady at the ice cream parlor, with whose name I am not favored, Joe Foster the clerk of our court, Frank Hicks our constable, Ed Westley the door man at the hotel, and others whom I can not call to mind begged to be commended to you.

*Our friend the Sheriff has just come to pay me a visit.
Upon my informing him that I was writing to you he at once
summoned Uncle Up and bade him serve us, "burn my cop-
pers" from my 1879 stock. We will partake of these to the
happy state of your affairs.*

*I heartily subscribe to the Sheriff's sentiment that neither
he nor I could hope or expect at our advanced age to meet
with a happier occasion for the employment of such vener-
able spirits.*

Permit me to subscribe myself,

Yours to command
Cavendish Culpepper

To
Master John Weatherford II
At the Town of Concord In New Hampshire

John Weatherford II
to
Judge Culpepper

My dear Judge Culpepper:
*I too present my compliments to you sir, and hope that
every single thing is just as nice with you as can be.*

*I have read your letter over ever so many times, but per-
haps won't be able to read it any more. Mr. Atwater saw me
looking at it this morning during the arithmetic class. I did
most awfully badly during that class and Mr. Atwater asked
me what I had been reading. When I told him what was in*

your letter and that I kept reading and reading it he said he thought he had better keep the letter till vacation started.

I would like to come back to La Marquisville and see you again more than anything in the whole world. Please sir, write my Uncle John just as soon as you can. Tell him how very much I want to come and tell him that I will be good and not bother you or talk at the table or lose my things, or be homesick on Christmas day, not visiting you, Sir.

I wonder if Uncle John will let Eddie come with me. Do you think he will? Should I write to him myself and tell him how much I want Eddie to come?

Oh dear, how can I stay at school two more whole weeks with all the things there are now to think about. Is my little horse still there, really? One of the very nicest things I do at school is to think about him when I first get into bed and pretend that we are hunting together.

Won't it be fun to see Uncle Up and Slim and Double Slim and my friend the Sheriff again and Joe Foster and the lady at the ice cream place and everybody.

Do you think we can read some more in the evenings? It's too bad that we finished Treasure Island. I don't suppose we could have Eddie with us when we read but it would be fun. Eddie was the first one I ever read to when I learned to read and I had to spell lots of words out to him and he told me what they were.

Thank you sir, very much for wanting me.

Your friend,
John

P.S.—Please write Uncle John just as quick as you can.

Colonel John Weatherford
to
John Weatherford II

My dear Nephew:

Judge Culpepper informs me that he has invited you to spend Christmas with him at La Marquisville.

I wish to impress upon you that the Judge pays you a notable compliment by this invitation, for he is indeed a very great gentleman.

If you feel sure that you wish to spend your holiday in Virginia and will be happy, and not lonesome on Christmas morning, then Aunt Tabitha and I will be delighted to have you visit with Judge Culpepper.

Aunt Tabitha writes me that your pony, Joseph Bigelow Thompson (I am informed that you resent the slightest abbreviation of his formidable nomenclature), has reached an age entitling him to sympathetic consideration in respect to the work he is called on to perform.

Age creeps on apace. Aunt Tabitha urges that you be given a horse more suitable to your age and experience on which to hunt and that Joseph Bigelow Thompson be reserved for hacking and less strenuous exertion. This would be a kindness to which his faithfulness entitles him.

In furtherance of this idea, and with the wish that you may have a new horse for Christmas morning, Aunt Tabitha and I have each contributed $250.

Judge Culpepper informs me that a serviceable light weight hunter may be procured for $500 in his less fashionable country. He further informs me that you went well on the horse he borrowed for you last year.

In so far as it is possible, I wish you to have the experience of initiating and completing this transaction yourself. With such in mind I enclose my check to Judge Culpepper's order in the sum of five hundred dollars. I do not draw it to you because of the complications incidental to you being a minor. Nor is it desirable to open a bank account with Judge Culpepper's bank because of the details involved. Ask Judge Culpepper to have the check cashed, then give the funds to Mr. Peckett at the bank, and have him place them in an envelope, suitably marked with your name. Mr. Peckett will give you the funds when and as you require them to consummate your purchase. Please show this letter to Judge Culpepper as his authority for assisting you.

I offer the following suggestions. In selecting and purchasing a horse, one that is to serve as a companion to you for perhaps many years, do not be hurried. Do not make your decision until you have seen and ridden whatever horses are available in the district. But in this connection do not ask an owner to saddle or name a price on a horse for you unless you are definitely interested in such horse. To do so is an imposition.

Do not buy a so-called made horse, unless you have hunted it in private.

In the matter of soundness, rely on Judge Culpepper's judgment.

To many people a horse is but a conveyance, to others a companion. You are of the latter class and it is therefore important that the horse's character and personality as proclaimed through his eyes and general expression should be appealing to you. Pay close attention to this.

And so dear Nephew, my affection and best wishes go with you for a happy holiday, crowned by a new horse for Christmas morning.

Affectionately,
Uncle John

John Weatherford II
to
Colonel John Weatherford

Dear Uncle John:
Not in all my life put together have I ever received so nice a letter as your last one; a horse for Christmas morning; a horse of my very own. I have thought and thought about how to write you a letter that would also be a nice one and would tell you the things I feel and keep thinking about. Why is it, Uncle John, that even when you are all excited so that you want, more than anything else, to put your arms around somebody who has been nice to you, you never can say anything or write anything except just something like "thank you very much." That doesn't tell how you feel, does it? Not really.

But perhaps you will remember when you were my age and maybe you had the same trouble.

I guess that all I can write is that your present and Aunt Tabitha's present is the wonderfulest thing that has ever happened to me and I thank you very much indeed. I will write Aunt Tabitha right away.

I know that Joseph Bigelow Thompson is getting old. Why last August and September before I went to school and while we were cubbing I never could get to the end of one single run. He and I have been such friends for so long that I couldn't ask him to trot up a hill if he didn't want to. And he doesn't like to jump now, not really. And yet, Uncle John, you don't know how he carries on if the other horses go hunting and he is left home.

All he really wants to do is to walk along looking at every-thing and everybody. When the Hunt leaves him behind, he will stand by himself the longest time, listening to hounds, and looking off to where their voices come from. Then when he thinks they are getting too far away, he will give a big sigh, sometimes it's sort of a grunt, and walk on.

Last year Eddie and I talked nearly every day about buying the horse I rode at La Marquisville. It's the most wonderful horse. Eddie thought we might be able to buy it in the installementation way. That means a little at a time, whenever you have any money you don't need for other things. I talked to Judge Culpepper and he said he was sure that the man would be very glad to do that for me. Then he asked me what my allowance was and we figured it all out on paper, and even if I didn't spend hardly anything for anything else, it came to sixteen years and on top of all those years, Uncle John, there were still eleven weeks of installementation. Judge Culpepper thought that the man was too old to sell the horse that way. He is sixty-eight years old and Judge Culpepper says that anyone that old in Virginia who hunts and uses new "corn" is apt to get a chill or something, nearly any time.

I will do just as you say about looking at all sorts of other horses and trying them, only you don't know how I feel about the horse I rode last year. Nobody knows.

Isn't it really wonderful about my going to Judge Culpepper's for Christmas? It was most awfully top hole of him to invite me.

Aren't you excited, Uncle John? You didn't say anything about Eddie in your letter. Of course there wouldn't be as much fun in Virginia, not nearly, without Eddie. It wouldn't be the same.

Have you seen him? Is he all excited the way I am? Did he talk much about La Marquisville? Has he still got the checked suit and checked cap that he likes so much?

Please, Uncle John, be very sure that Eddie has lots of money for himself when he comes. I don't need any, but nobody but me knows how much trouble poor Eddie has all the time about his money. He has to take the young lady in the candy store to the movies, sometimes as far as Harroldsburg. He has to buy special food for his game chickens and some of it is meat. Then he has to get his checked suit pressed ever so often. And there are lots of other things.

Eddie was always wishing he had a new pair of leggins, pigskin ones. Please Uncle John, don't you think you could get him a pair. He likes to dress up very nicely when he hunts. Why Mr. Clark put a piece in the La Marquisville paper that said something like this, "Mr. Edward Patrick Walsh, the well known horseman understands how a sporting man should dress and turn himself out. Our local bow broomhills would do well to observe him." Wasn't that very nice, Uncle John?

All I can think about is my new horse. I do hope that every single thing is very nice with you.

With lots of love,
John

Colonel Weatherford
to
John Weatherford II

Dear Nephew:
In reply to your letter. I cannot even consider permitting Walsh to go with you at this time. I have not spoken to him

about La Marquisville and do not know whether he is excited or what his feelings may be. His money, what he does with it, his articles of attire, the special diet for his game cocks as well as his social engagements with the young person in the candy store are his own concerns. Most certainly so.

Yours truly,
Uncle John

Colonel Weatherford
to
John Weatherford II

Dear Nephew:
   I received your day letter telegram about Walsh going to Virginia with you. It contained 163 words. To say that I am put out and annoyed is stating it mildly.
   Such disregard for your Aunt Tabitha's money is reprehensible in the extreme.
   Quite apart from this phase, I had to send a car twenty-five miles to Poughkeepsie and twenty-five miles back again to procure the message, it having arrived on Sunday and being too long and too unintelligible to take over the telephone.
   No. Walsh can not accompany you. I have pressing need for him here.

Yours truly,
Uncle John

P.S. If you purpose electing the profligate course of sending 163 word telegrams, God bless me, learn to break them by interjecting the word "stop" at suitable intervals. Such a jumble of words and ideas running into each other I never saw. A solid hour of an otherwise pleasant Sunday morning was completely wasted in trying to make head or tail of the message.

John Weatherford II
to
Colonel John Weatherford M.F.H.

My dear Uncle John,
    Oh, I feel so badly about the telegram and it being too long, and not having any of those stops, which I didn't know about before and you having to send the car so far. It just seems that everything I did, I did wrong.
    But please Uncle John I don't want you to feel badly about Aunt Tabitha's money. It really wasn't Aunt Tabitha's money I spent on the telegram. I have a dollar a week, spending money, and haven't used hardly any of it this term or last term. I have been saving up to buy my dog Hiccup a nice kennel, the kind that has a porch at the front so a dog can be in the shade. They cost ten dollars without the porch and twelve dollars with the porch. I just took a part of this money for the telegram because I wanted Eddie to come to Virginia with me so very, very much and I can easily save some more before the hot weather comes and Hiccup needs the porch. I didn't know how you needed Eddie or I wouldn't have sent the telegram. La Marquisville is really quite a long way from

home and I sort of wanted Eddie when Christmas Day comes.
I am very sorry again that I made you any trouble and
didn't use the stops.

Love,
John

Telegram
Col. John Weatherford
to
John Weatherford II

*Extremely sorry I wrote you so abruptly about your telegram
and about Walsh Stop He will come to the school motor you
to Judge Culpepper's and remain there Stop Am sending you
a terrier kennel with front shade porch and a portrait of a rat
painted over the entrance so that Hiccup will feel at home
Stop Walsh has a pair of new leggins, pigskin, and all neces-
sary money for candy lady and meat for cocks Stop He is extremely excited about the trip talks volubly about it and reports that checked suit and cap are in good order.*

With affection and good wishes
Uncle John

Telegram
John Weatherford II
to
Colonel John Weatherford M.F.H.

Dear Uncle Stop thank you very much for letting Stop Eddie Stop come with me and thank you for Hiccup's Kennel and Eddie's leggins and Stop everything love.

John

Judge Culpepper
to
Colonel Weatherford

My dear Colonel:
John arrived this morning in high spirits. He did me the honor of confiding the purport of your letter to him about his purchasing a horse for Christmas. You have my assurance that the little affair in hand will have my best thought and attention.

I would not have you think, my dear Colonel, that the years have gone too far in softening me but I do confess that my emotions came near to getting the better of me, what with the boy's pure joy and happiness, and one thing or another. Is it that such demonstrations—the look in youth's eyes, the glow of a clean, happy heart, the love of life as it is at the moment awaken once more, in young old people like you and me, memories of our own boyhood?

All of those who saw John out hunting last year on the

little chestnut horse I borrowed for him were struck by and commented upon the rare affinity between horse and rider. As you know, it was the boy's first experience over a big country, yet it would have taxed any one in our field to have hung him up. His confidence in the horse and the horse's confidence in him was complete.

I had thought never to mention the following little incident but its telling may augment your pleasure in giving him the horse.

On the last evening of his previous visit with me we were reading Mr. Stevenson's splendid tale, Treasure Island, *aloud. I happened to look up and was perturbed to note that John was, well, I was going to write crying. Let us rather say, that a tear had slipped out of covert. When he saw me looking at him he stood up, said, "Excuse me, Sir" and left the room. I closed the book and the Sheriff and I conversed. In a few moments John returned and we finished the chapter.*

After the Sheriff had left us I made bold to assure John that whereas I did not wish to enquire regarding his personal affairs yet he had my every assurance that my counsels were his to command.

He smiled, then broke into a laugh, saying, "It was very foolish of me, Sir. I know I'm too old to do such a thing but while you were reading I started thinking about this being my last night here, and felt badly about leaving you and everybody and then thought that perhaps I would never come back to La Marquisville in my very whole life.

"On top of all that I started wondering about my little horse. I guess that was too much, Sir. It was remembering the times when we both got so tired and how he kept up on his feet and never let me down.

"When you are feeling this way, sir, why you sort of make up most awfully bad things to think about. Just as you looked at me I was thinking that my little horse might be sold to

*some one, perhaps too heavy for him to carry. He is really
very small, and the next second I saw him trying to climb a
big hill and keep up and, and, well anyway, sir, I was very
babyish but I won't do it again, ever."*

*Pray do me the kindness my dear Colonel of not mentiong
the fact that I related this confidential little passage to you.*

*Rest assured that John will have a horse for Christmas
morning and a good one.*

I subscribe myself,

Yours to command
Cavendish Culpepper

JOHN WEATHERFORD—HIS NOTE BOOK

Eddie and I are in La Marquisville again and I have seen my
little horse. He is just the same, just exactly. We drove all
night. Eddie said, "It is rediciloose, positively by all manner
o' means, you and me wasting time by spending a night at a
hotel and maybe missing some good huntin'. We are goin'
straight through from Boston to Virginia."

When it got dark Eddie made me move into the back of
the car. He fixed a pillow out of my saddle and told me to
"look sharp, mind what I was about and go to sleep." I
wasn't very sleepy and didn't want to go to sleep but sort of
pretended to be. Eddie whistled and sang Irish songs to himself and every once in a while he would talk to the car. "Roll
on old bus," he'd say. "Roll on down to Virginia. Roll down

to those big stone walls, to those long legged, romping foxes, to those hundred acre fields, to those man-killing colts of Judge Culpepper's. Give her a whisp of extra gas, Eddie, for the young lady in the candy shop. This is the life, rolling south a'huntin'." Eddie can talk to himself the most of anybody I ever knew, more than even my friend Mr. Sweatser, the lobster man at Framingham.

Judge Culpepper is coming now so I can't write any more in my book.

It's the evening now. Oh, but I have had such a wonderful day. Every single thing was wonderful.

In the morning we went schooling, Judge Culpepper, Eddie and me, and I rode my horse. He is mine, even if he isn't quite yet.

Eddie had a most awfully bad time, riding what Judge Culpepper said was the worst jumper he had ever owned, or seen, or even heard about. The Judge has spent two years trying to teach the horse to jump but he just doesn't learn.

Why, this horse never even looks at a jump till he is right under it, then twists himself over, hits the fence hard, and nearly always pecks when he lands.

Judge Culpepper said the horse was too bad to sell to anybody and ever so much too good looking and nice mannered to feed to the hounds.

Well, like it always is when you are with Eddie, something sort of exciting started. He asked Judge Culpepper if it would be all right if he were to turn the horse over and give him something to think about. The Judge told him to go ahead and try but that no one could turn that horse over, because he had practiced hitting his fences so long.

We rode on and pretty soon Eddie pointed to a fence in another field that he said was very beautiful because it was big, and strong, and had lots of briars for a horse to fall in, if he thought he would rather fall than stand up.

When we came to the fence it was so high that Judge Culpepper didn't think that the horse would even try to jump it. But Eddie said that if I would give him a lead he thought he could get his horse to either jump it or fall over it.

Judge Culpepper was on a beautiful three-year-old that had hardly ever jumped anything, so I was the only one who could give Eddie a lead. It was a most awfully big fence.

Judge Culpepper looked at it quite a long time then said, "Go on, John, my boy, have a try at it."

My little horse saw from a long ways off that it was a very high fence and was ready. He jumped it wonderfully, and oh, how he felt under me! When I think about it a long time it seems as though I feel about this horse just the way I do about my sister Aleece and my brother Cabot. Perhaps this isn't right but I can't help it.

I could hear Eddie coming back of me and quick as anything I began feeling all wabbly or empty or something inside, thinking about Eddie maybe falling down in all those briars, perhaps under the horse and getting hurt. I looked back. He seemed to be coming very slowly. Then all of a sudden his whip started. He was using it on both sides, back of the saddle. No one can use a whip as fast as Eddie but he hardly ever uses one.

The horse jumped forward. He was close to the fence. Eddie drove him towards the post. It all happened most awfully fast. The horse's hind feet were away up in the air to the right of the post and down he and Eddie crashed. Eddie went into the briars, head first, but was up in a second, pulled the horse up on his feet, mounted and took his checked cap off to see if it was all right.

Judge Culpepper had watched everything from the other side of the fence, then he came through a gate. All he said to Eddie was, "Walsh! Are you a married man?" Eddie told him he wasn't.

Eddie jumped the horse over six more small fences and Judge Culpepper said that no one in the whole State of Virginia would ever believe it was the same horse. Why, he went to the jumps with his ears forward, watching everything and jumped straight and careful and didn't even tick one of the fences. Then we rode home. Isn't my friend Eddie the wonderfulest horseman?

In the afternoon I went to the candy store, the bank, the courthouse, and the hotel and the hardware store, to see my friends. It was fun. They all said that they felt very well indeed and every single one of them said that they hoped that I would have a nice Christmas in La Marquisville. I told them about my going to get a new horse for Christmas.

They were all getting ready for Christmas themselves, all except poor Hezakia Up, the old colored man who used to train Judge Culpepper's game-cocks, when the Judge was young.

Hezakia lost his son yesterday, the one he liked the best, and when I went to his cabin, his daughter said that he was all broken up and wouldn't eat or see anybody but just sat in a corner all day long, rocking himself.

Well, anyway, I decided to go in and see him. It was quite dark inside but pretty soon I could see Hezakia, rocking back and forth, moaning, and tears were running down his cheeks. He felt, oh, so terribly badly. He was trimming a game-cock for Mr. Churchill.

We are great friends and talked about lots of things. He gave me his turtle shell, the big one that Mrs. Up used as a cradle for all their children.

I asked Hezakia if it would be all right for me to lend the shell to Mrs. Double Slim because she has a new baby.

He said that it would be all right and that turtle shells made the best cradles in the world for colored babies; that when his children were little he used to tie a piece of string to the side of the turtle shell, run the string through a hook in the ceiling and tie the other end of the string to the rocker of his chair. He told me that he had trimmed maybe a thousand game-cocks for La Marquisville gentlemen while rocking the turtle shell.

I think Mrs. Double Slim will like it very much.

Judge Culpepper received a letter this morning from Gen. Olcott asking if I would like to go rabbit shooting with him in the afternoon. I said I would like most awfully to go.

General Olcott has a wooden leg but hunts and shoots nearly every day. He likes rabbit shooting better than any other sport, mostly because he has bred a small sort of rabbit hound all his life and has great fun seeing them work and listening to their voices.

Judge Culpepper told me that General Olcott was the most old-fashioned gentleman of all Virginia in the way he talks and thinks and writes and does things, and that it is because he spends most of his time reading about the Duke of Marl-borough and fighting all the Duke's battles over and over and over again.

The Judge said that I should copy the General's letter in my book which I do right now. It was nice of him to want me to shoot with him. This is the letter.

"General Olcott presents his compliments to Judge Cul-pepper and wishes to inquire whether his guest, Master Weatherford would be pleased to attend upon the La Mar-quisville rabbits this afternoon at three by the clock. If so, he will be waited upon at such hour.

"That gentlemen of Virginia do not accord rabbit shooting the favor it deserves is due to a shocking lack of knowledge regarding the sport. They neither observe the niceties nor practice the proprieties of this ancient pursuit, one highly regarded by His Grace the Duke of Marlborough while campaigning in Spain. His Grace truthfully remarked that to go a-rabbiting raised the expectations yet left the gratification an uncertainty; a prerequisite of good sport.

"It is believed that young Master Weatherford will enjoy and be instructed through watching the hounds questioning for the rabbits and listening to their merry cry which bespeaks them to be on the scent.

"General Olcott subscribes himself to be Judge Culpepper's obliged and obedient servant, to command."

General Olcott came for me with a mule team. He wore a high grey hat they call a beaver and a green coat, a kind of coat I had never seen before, very long and double breasted, with big white buttons. His necktie was black and went around his neck two or three times and then puffed out.

It's not so easy for a boy to get used to General Olcott or feel comfortable with him at first.

Hi Up, who was dressed in a soldier's old faded uniform drove the mules and we sat in the back seat. The General sits with his wooden leg stuck out in front of him on a box. He doesn't call Hi Up by his name but always says Serg. Major, and every time he does it Hi Up salutes. When we came to a good road the General said, "Serg. Major, we will traverse this terrain at double time" and Hi Up saluted, then poked the mules with the handle of the whip and they trotted. Once General Olcott told Hi to halt the transport wagon, took his leg down, stood up and looked over the country for a long time. I thought he was wondering about a good place to shoot. Pretty soon he asked me to stand up and pointed to a big, bare hill with some woods on one side and said, "Master

Weatherford, a small complement of the Duke's infantry, properly deployed in those woods, commanded by officers of spirit, could have maintained their position against a formidable number of cavalry, certainly three troops, possibly four. Attention, Serg. Major, advance."

A little while after that we came to the place where we were to shoot. General Olcott took one hound called Marshall Ney out of the dog crate, and told Hi that he was to make a quick reconnaissance and then conceal the escort wagon behind some bushes.

When Hi came back General Olcott said, "Serg. Major, you will serve as orderly to Master Weatherford who will shoot the east side of the hedgerow. I will take up my position to the west and maintain it at all hazards. We will advance."

The hedgerow was about sixty feet wide and covered with briars and small bushes. Marshall Ney worked down the center of it very carefully.

There is one thing I certainly learned and that is if you are going to shoot rabbits out of a hedgerow you have to shoot quickly. Why the rabbits bounced out like hard served tennis balls. I missed three, one right after another.

I called to General Olcott and asked him if I could please come over on his side for a little while. I told him about the trouble I was having and that I wanted to watch him. He had shot four times and had four rabbits. We went on. A rabbit bounced out and the General bowled it over. Why, he didn't even bring the gun to his shoulder, only up to about his waist, and fired the second he saw the rabbit.

I went back to my side of the hedge, but didn't think there would be any sense of me trying to aim from my waist but I did try to shoot a lot faster. I missed the next four rabbits but got the fifth one.

We hunted for two hours, walking one hedgerow after another. The General shot all the rabbits that the law would let him but I only shot three and missed ever so many.

It was getting dark then so the General told Hi to bring up the convoy wagon and that we would retire to the general staff headquarters at La Marquisville for the night.

Driving home I asked General Olcott how I could learn to shoot better—what I should do. He told me that rabbit shooting out of hedgerows was snap shooting, that you had to take snap shots; that it was much harder than quail shooting because when dogs once came to a point on quail it made you get ready to shoot but that you never knew when a rabbit was going to charge at you out of a hedgerow and therefore you had to be ready every single second, and it was hard for most people to keep their minds on the rabbits and keep ready every second.

I asked him how I could learn to keep my mind on the rabbits and be always ready. He said that I would have to pretend that I was a very young officer fighting with the Duke of Marlborough in Spain; that the rabbits were the King's enemies; that the Duke of Marlborough and his staff were watching me from a high hill; that I wanted to be mentioned in the Gazette and promoted and so must bring down every enemy who rushed at me from the hedgerow; that it would help if I would make up nice things that were printed in the Gazette and that one of them might be, "His Grace the Duke of Marlborough was pleased to mention the dashing courage of Captain John Weatherford II of the Cold Stream Guards, who, single handed and under intense fire cleared an important salient between San Sebastian and El Porto of the enemy."

And the General said that when he was younger he used to pretend that the war in Spain was all over and that the army was back in England; that there was a great victory parade in London and that he was now a Colonel of the Cold Stream Guards and was riding on a very handsome grey horse right back of the Duke of Marlborough when they marched past Buckingham Palace. Why the General said that a rabbit in a Virginia hedgerow didn't have a chance of getting away when he was all excited and thinking about those wonderful things and that he could hit a grasshopper just as easy as a rabbit.

He said that now, when he had trouble keeping his mind on the rabbits he just pretended that he was the Duke of Marlborough himself, but that it would be very disrespectful for me to do that.

I didn't do anything that was really awfully wrong, except that twice I got to the windward of the rabbits and I can see now that this spoils the shooting. It was all such fun.

General Olcott said I was to put a penny up on the wall of my bedroom and sight my gun just as fast as I could on the penny twenty-five times in the morning and twenty-five times before I went to bed.

I tried two horses today, just because I promised Uncle John I would. One fell, over a very little fence, and the other went away with me for pretty near a whole mile. I didn't think they were awfully good, not really.

Everything is getting Christmasy at Judge Culpepper's and all over La Marquisville. It's really pretty exciting. Today Uncle Up told Mr. Waithcock, he is Judge Culpepper's superintendent, that we had to have five turkeys, big ones, for Christmas dinner at our house.

After Uncle Up and I talked a long time about Christmas I didn't feel awfully good, not really. I've never been away from Aunt Tabitha's and my brother and sister at Christmas. Maybe it would be better not to think or write any more about that.

I wonder if it is all right, when you feel sort of lonesome, to want, most of anything, to go out to a stable and visit a horse. Maybe that's queer and silly. But anyway, when I get thinking about Christmas and home, the only place that makes me feel better is my little horse's box stall.

If I have to send this notebook to Uncle John to read, I guess I had better take this page out.

I sort of wish I hadn't told Eddie about my aiming my gun every morning and evening at pennies because now, no matter how tired I am at night or how sleepy I am in the morning, he makes me do all that sighting.

Eddie didn't think one penny was any good because he said Uncle John always brought down a brace of birds, so we now have two pennies stuck in chewing gum on the wall. After a couple of days, Eddie, just like he always does about everything, got excited at this penny sighting and said he should practice being a loader for me because we might go to Scotland to shoot next year. Well, he borrowed an old gun from somebody; my, but it's heavy!

He makes me stand at the foot of the bed, with him right back of me, and says he is a beater and a loader all in one. Suddenly he calls out, so loud that you could hear him clear over at the stable, "Mark right" or "Mark left," "Hi cock," then makes a whirring kind of noise like a bird makes with its wings and I shoot at one of the pennies, then the other one and Eddie always says, "Both down, Master John. Both down," and shoves the big gun at me and by that time he is so excited he can hardly talk and reloads as fast as he can and shouts, "Birds coming over, all directions. Give 'em the works, Master John. Another brace. Haven't missed a bird." He goes on this way till I have sighted twenty-five times.

Once he called out, "You, you Scotchman, get out of the way, or lie down." And another time he got into a most awful row with some man, whom Eddie said was shooting at my birds. My, the things Eddie called the man and the things he said he was going to do to him just as soon as I had finished shooting. He counts the birds every time we shoot. He used to start at a hundred but he starts a lot higher than that now. When he has finished counting he waves his hand and says, "Now then Sandy, my lad, look sharp. Pack and send these birds to the Dundas Hospital and mind you mark them with the compliments of Master John Weatherford II and don't steal any, and send Jock to the glen to bring up Master John's riding pony. Look sharp, my man."

I go to bed and Eddie picks up the guns, blows through the barrels, just as though they had been shot through, wipes everything off with his handkerchief, says "All spick and span, ready for Glen Aldie in the morning" and goes down to see the young lady in the candy store. It's funny that he never gets tired or sleepy but has fun all the time. He even has fun cleaning a saddle or a pair of shoes. He told me the other day that he wouldn't trust a man around the corner that didn't take the laces out of a pair of shoes before he cleaned the shoes.

He says that a gentleman's saddle has to be as clean as a pocket book and that if a gentleman's breeches ever got dirty from a saddle that he had cleaned, he would buy the gentleman a new pair of breeches.

Eddie and I tried four horses today. When it was all over, Eddie sat down on a bale of hay, put his head in his hands and didn't say anything for a long time, then said, "If you and me keep on trying these horses we are going to get killed, by all manner o' means, whatsoever, positively."

One of my knees and one of my ankles are quite a little sore and Eddie's left cheek looks, well he says it looks as though he had been careless with some wild-cats.

Of all the people I have ever heard read, Judge Culpepper is the best. We are reading *Oliver Twist* out loud in the evenings. Once, when the Sheriff and I were alone the Sheriff said to me, "John, that Mr. Dickens thought he was a very fine writer. Why the conceited old rascal. It's nothing but the Judge's reading. It is his reading that makes me want to put a bullet in that scoundrel Fagin. And soup, John, soup, filthy, watery soup. Do you remember the rascal who ran the poorhouse and wouldn't give Oliver a second cup of the —— —— muck. I'll tell you boy, walking home that night I gave that workhouse fellow such a hiding with my cane that my arm pained. Mr. Dickens is nothing at all, nothing at all. It's just my valued old friend's reading that makes the story worth listening to."

My but we had a fine read last night. Twice Judge Culpepper stopped reading because he said it was time for me to go to bed but both times it was in very exciting places and I asked him please wouldn't he read just a little longer. The Sheriff was as excited as I was and said, "—— it, you old fossil, go on! Go on with the story! What's the matter with those London policemen? Haven't they a Sheriff? I thought they had a Lord High Sheriff of London. —— —— the man, where is he? Drunk at some chop house I suppose."

Then he pulled out his revolver and sighted on two little blue cupids fixed to the top of Judge Culpepper's clock. He crossed his legs, rested his elbow on one knee and took a most awfully careful, long aim. Then he said, "It won't do. It can't be done. Here boy, change chairs with me. Don't dawdle." He sat down in my chair, took another long aim, then said, so loud that Judge Culpepper had to stop reading, "There, I have a bead on both of them." Judge Culpepper asked him what all the trouble was about and who he had such a nice bead on and he said that the Cupid on the left was Fagin and the other one was the man in the workhouse who wouldn't give poor little Oliver Twist some more soup.

Judge Culpepper was a little cross and said, "Well, pick them both off quickly, so that John and I can get on with the story. We are excited."

The Sheriff, only because the Judge wanted him to, wouldn't get finished with his shooting but said he would just keep his eye on both of the ——ed rascals.

Judge Culpepper went on with the story and the Sheriff was nice and quiet but every once in a while he would whip the pistol out of his pocket, quickly, and that made Judge Culpepper sort of jumpy.

Then we came to the place where old Fagin stole the handkerchief out of the man's pocket to show Oliver how you would pick a pocket. The Judge was reading and I was listening and it was very quiet, when both Judge Culpepper and I jumped and the Judge's glasses fell off. The Sheriff had hollered out, "Got both of them. Now Fagin, my man, I'll put you where there are no pockets to pick. And you—you soup hoarder. Ha, Ha."

The Judge said he thought things were getting too mixed up, to read any more tonight. Then he asked the Sheriff what was the sense of picking off important people in the first part of a story; that it spoiled the story for us to have Fagin wounded and locked up, right at that part of the story. All the Sheriff would say was that if we were sheriffs we would understand those sort of things better. He rang for a night cap. When I started for bed I heard him tell the Judge that he never shot better than he did tonight and the Judge said he was very glad to hear it.

We ran three foxes this morning and accounted for every single one. The last fox ran so fast and so far and in such a hilly country that none of the horses could hunt any longer.

Eddie got a fall, Dr. Prentice got one and so did Mr. Stringfellow. The Sheriff's cranky roan horse started to go off with him in some woods and the Sheriff lost the whole top of his hunting hat when the horse ran him under a low branch. I was right behind him and he turned around and shook his fist at me and said, "You, you, you wretched brat of a boy get away from here and give me room to talk to this horse. Ride up the path—ride any place but do it quickly."

Well, a lot of gentlemen came back to our house for luncheon. Uncle Up and George and Anthony Jackson all had their plum colored liveries and brass buttons. Right in the very middle of luncheon the Sheriff stood up and told everybody to stop talking and be quiet. Then he turned to me and said, "My deah young friend, you accommodated me this morning while we were afield. The matter I had in hand permitted of no delay. I apologize, Suh, for my lack of civility and give myself the pleasure of drinking your health."

In the afternoon I had to try three horses. They were no good, but I knew they wouldn't be.

After that Major Padget and I went crow shooting.

I had a dream about my own little horse last night, the one I am going to buy. I guess it's too foolish to put in my book but I would sort of like to.

I was back at Aunt Tabitha's and it was time to go to school only I couldn't find my home work and it was very important home work, at least it was to me.

The car was waiting and everybody was telling me to hurry and that the car couldn't wait because Weatherall had to get Aunt Tabitha to the train. Mary and Meg and the butler, Saunders, were all sort of pushing me towards the door. They said Aunt Tabitha was getting cross.

I just had to find my homework and was pushing back. Then all at once my little horse was right in front of me and he walked over to the couch and shoved away a pillow with his muzzle. As soon as he touched the pillow I remembered that I had put my homework under it the night before when I went upstairs to bed. I woke right up then and that was all there was to the dream. I'm glad it was my horse that helped me, and found the homework and not one of the dogs or somebody else. It didn't seem funny to have a horse, not that horse, in Aunt Tabitha's library, not really.

I think it's too bad that people heard about my going to buy a horse and too bad that I promised Uncle John to look at different horses. Eleven horses came to our place today and it was raining hard.

The only good part about it is that Eddie has such fun. He gets the owners talking about how wonderful and how high their horses can jump, then says, "All right, all right, now then, now then we will see about this business," and he climbs up on the horses and heads them down to Judge Culpepper's white board fence which is four foot four inches high.

This may be fun for Eddie and Slim and Double Slim and the boys in the stable who all stand around and laugh and call out to Eddie but it is not any fun for me.

I think I have looked at enough horses and had better get the money from Mr. Beckett and buy my own little horse before Eddie gets hurt, and besides, Christmas is pretty near here. I wish I could think of what to get Eddie and Uncle Up and Judge Culpepper and my great friend the Sheriff, and Slim and everybody for Christmas. I think it would be very nice indeed if people had more money at Christmas than they do have.

While I was thinking about my little horse the other day I thought it would be fun to give him a new halter for Christmas, a good one, all for himself. I talked to Eddie and he thought it was a most awfully good idea, and said he would write to New York for one.

My but Eddie has fun doing everything he does. As soon as I told him about the halter he said, "All right, all right. That's it. That's it. A princess type is the thing, an English one, four rows of stitching, solid brass buckles, brass name plate. What's the horse's name? Must put name of sire and dam on name plate. Look smart. Come with me."

We went to see Mr. Harkaway who owns the horse. He said that it didn't have a real name but that everybody just called it Harkaway's little horse; that its sire was Ganadore and its mother's name was Betty Y. I asked Mr. Harkaway if he would mind my calling the horse Harkaway and he said, "Suh, it would please me. Will you honor my house and join me in a glass of Elderberry wine?"

On the way home I asked Eddie what the halter would cost. He figured it up and said that with the name plate and writing all the letters, and a leather brow-band, and white one and a shank with brass chain at the end and everything, he thought it would cost about seven dollars.

I didn't know what to do. I haven't got that much money but I didn't want to make Eddie feel bad. Anyway, when we got home I had to tell Eddie that I couldn't buy a halter like that. He was very nice and said that it was a lot of money, that he and I had always been very poor, but that we had more fun than any other people he knew and that we should be thankful about lots of things.

Eddie thought that the thing to do was to buy the brass name plate with the names all written on it this Christmas and maybe next Christmas get a brow band, and each Christmas get some other part and pretty soon I would have the whole halter. That's what I am going to do.

I'm glad I stopped looking at and trying different horses. It didn't seem fair to my own little horse, not really. It was— well I don't know just what it was but it wasn't fair and square to him. It was just as though I thought that maybe there might be some other horse just as good or better than he is.

Eddie says that it might spoil Christmas if I bought the horse right now and that I should wait till just the very day before Christmas, and that I am not to look at him from the time I buy him till Christmas morning. Eddie wants to do his mane up in a very special way with a little bit of holly at the top of each braid.

I am not going to write any more in my book, not till I get home. Nobody but me knows how long it takes, and I have so much to do. You can't write in a book when you are sleepy, not really. Eddie doesn't see why I get sleepy because he never does, but it makes you sleepy in the evening if you fox hunt or go quail shooting seven and eight hours nearly every day, and sometimes shoot crows in between, and maybe try a couple of horses and then listen to Judge Culpepper read after dinner.

Three times I have gone sound asleep while writing in my book in bed and Eddie found the light burning when he came in the morning to wake me. He didn't like it very much.

I am going to try hard to remember all I can about my visit and will write it in the book when I am back at school.

Judge Culpepper
to
Colonel Weatherford

My dear Colonel:
You have my every assurance that I would not write you in the manner following were I not concerned regarding your nephew. The responsibility for his well being is, of course, mine, while he is my guest.

True, I have but little first hand knowledge of the youth of today, but this has not prevented me from observing during the last few days what I may only characterize as an unhappy change in the boy's conduct and management of his affairs. He appears to me and to his other friends here, secretive and only half interested in the riding, hunting and shooting. A shocking state of affairs in a gentleman.

After trying a formidable array of horses, brought here

for his inspection, which in number looked to me to be the outpouring of half of the State of Virginia, he finally settled upon the purchase of the fine little horse he has been hunting. He could not have done better. No more courageous, gallant animal ever looked through the bridle. I would have been deeply distressed had John let this horse escape him.

But, my dear Colonel, he has not consummated the purchase. Christmas is but a few days off and I have assumed that both his Aunt Tabitha and yourself wish him to have the horse for Christmas morning.

I sometimes wonder whether I should not charge myself with neglect for not looking more carefully into the association between Walsh and John, but knowing well how meticulous you are about those in your employ I have given the matter no thought.

Recently, however, John has been going off with Walsh, spending an entire morning or afternoon, once an entire day. Perhaps they spend too much time at the movies, or with Walsh's game chickens.

It has been our custom, while the boy is here, to read aloud in the early evening. The Sheriff always joins us. During the past year I have looked back fondly to such evenings.

This year, at the Sheriff's suggestion, I have been reading Oliver Twist *aloud. Whereas John sits quietly and respectfully his mind seems not on the book or even in the room. A week ago he was engrossed by the tale. True, the Sheriff is at times very disconcerting. When, in the story, acts of lawlessness are touched upon, the realism of Mr. Dickens' writing affects the Sheriff and he makes uncomfortably free with his fire-arms, but this is no novel sight to John.*

I trust you will understand me if I suggest that possibly Walsh's present influence may not be good for the boy. I do indeed hesitate to write this because personally I have thought well of Walsh and everyone here who saw him last year noted his solicitude for the boy and the sensible care of him in the field and in all other situations. Might it not be that a line from you to the boy would be all that is required. I am so devoted to him, as we all are, that I must guard against any ill befalling him.

Faithfully,
Cavendish Culpepper

Colonel Weatherford
to
John Weatherford II

Dear Nephew:
   A letter from Judge Culpepper causes me to be highly displeased with your present conduct and manner of employing your time at La Marquisville. It appears that you have chosen to spend most of your hours with Walsh, neglecting the rare opportunity, an opportunity not given to many boys of your age, of being in the company with gentlemen of the old school. There are but few of them left. La Marquisville is the only place I know in which they have survived in any number. This is because the town holds out no commercial attractions.
   And here you are, spending the days of your vacation with a harrum scarrum, cock fighting, irresponsible Irish groom. I am of a mind to wire you to start home with Walsh immediately and would do so were I not fearful that such course would be upsetting to your Aunt Tabitha. I have under ad-

visement wiring Walsh to come home and you to follow by train at the conclusion of your visit.

Remember, I shall expect to hear more satisfactory reports of your behavior.

Yours truly,
John Weatherford

Telegram
Colonel Weatherford
to
Judge Culpepper

Have written John but if he continues to give you concern send him home immediately Stop Walsh has been a trial to me for twenty years and will undoubtedly continue such Stop Deeply regret the apprehension and worry you have been subjected to Stop Christmas greetings

John Weatherford

Judge Culpepper
to
Colonel Weatherford

My dear Colonel and honored friend:
I write this at a late hour of Christmas night. Those dear old friends, in whose pleasant company I have spent so many

happy Christmas days, have wended their way homeward to their own hearths. I am alone in my library. In this room I have spent each of my 74 Christmases, my father spent all of his and my grandfather the last 46 of his. The spirit of the Culpeppers has indeed seeped deeply into the crevices of these walls.

How, my dear Colonel, am I to tell you of this Christmas Day. May I preface by bespeaking your indulgence if I write at too great length. I am not a trained writer, yet things of the heart ask to be told. But to progress.

It has been my custom for years to invite many of my old friends, with their ladies and such of their families as may be with them to dine with me at three of the clock on Christmas afternoon.

In these less formal days I have abandoned the use of the Culpepper plate but do make a point of using it at Christmas. In spite of the vicissitudes of life and of family I am still able to seat forty-eight guests before plate made for the Culpepper family seat in Yorkshire in 1573. This year we were to sit forty-six at table.

In order that we may have leisure to compose ourselves, visit one with another, and enter into the spirit of the occasion I ask my guests to join me at two o'clock.

Perhaps you are now able to envisage the scene in my library as it was on this Christmas day. Stories were being told, healths drunk and personal anecdotes revived from long past years, were being recalled. Much harmless banter was passing from one to another.

Suddenly, in the midst of this gay, happy scene my butler, Uncle Up, announced that a Mr. and Mrs. Carter Pembrook were calling upon me. The name had all but passed from my memory but by the time I reached the reception room I recalled the family. What was my amazement, upon going forward to meet them, to find them disposing of their outer garments, evidently preparing for a stay of some duration, and my dear Colonel, this was followed by protestation of appreciation of my having invited them to Christmas dinner, they and their three small children.

To better acquaint you with the situation I digress a moment to enlarge upon this family. They are gentle folk of the very first water to whom fortune and life has been indeed cruel. They live on the extreme edge of our hunting country, have no ties with La Marquisville or its people and have been practically forgotten here. They have withdrawn from all social intercourse due to the extreme poverty in which they live. It has been known in a general way that they were in difficulties but until today none of us had the slightest intimation that they or any family in our neighborhood was in such a plight.

Pembrook himself is a handsome, prematurely aged man. No vice or indiscretions have ever been assigned to him. He is an engaging companion but perchance a bad manager of his own affairs. His wife is a person of distinction and charm but haggard and emaciated, through, I suppose, self denial. The children are courteous of manner and even in their scanty and tragic garments are distinguished, a girl of four, another girl of seven and the oldest boy of perhaps ten.

No words of mine could describe the destitute appearance of this family. The boy had no shoes, even at this Christmas season. Pembrook's own clothes were neatly patched with sacking from a feed bag. I lack heart to even try to describe the appearance of Mrs. Pembrook or her daughters.

I would not wish you to charge me with lacking the spirit of hospitality or forgetting what the attitude of Him whose birthday we were celebrating would have been. "In as much as you did it unto one of the least of these, you did it unto me." But I must confess to having been perplexed.

While endeavoring to collect myself and formulate some suitable plan, a disturbance of another character broke forth.

I was conscious of all the dogs on the place giving uproarious tongue.

I excused myself for a moment thinking to quiet them. At the front door, a sight met me which I will endeavor to describe.

Coming up the driveway approaching the house was one of my farm wagons, which had been entirely covered with some white cotton material to resemble snow. Hitched to the wagon were six of my white mules each equipped with a set of jerk-team bells. Countless red balls made from red yarn had been attached to the harness by white strings.

On the seat sat a conventional Santa Claus, red coat, white beard, high cap and all the rest, including the generous waist band. Accompanying Santa Claus on the driver's seat was an elfin looking character, one that I did not recall in connection with the Christmas season.

The back of the wagon was seemingly filled but with what I could not then determine. Attached to the rear of the wagon, my dear Colonel, was a stone-bolt on which stood a barrel or rather half a barrel, serving as a stand for a Christmas tree, completely and handsomely decorated.

The entire colored population of my farms with their visitors and relations numbering probably 150, were following or surrounding the wagon, clapping and laughing, the younger children verging on hysterics.

The bells, the barking of the dogs, and uproarious clamor of the colored people had brought my guests out to the terrace.

Upon reaching the house, the six mules were brought to a halt with a tremendous flourish, the portly Santa Claus singing out, "Whoa Donner and Blitzen and all you reindeer. Whoa, Whoa." Then standing up in the wagon he demanded to know in a loud voice whether Ann, Enid, and Algerton Pembrook were at this house.

One would think that I had lived too long and seen too

*much and too many sides of life to be emotionally touched,
but it would seem not. I turned and saw the three frail little
children pressed shyly against the front of the house, the
sisters holding each others' hands. The boy's alert handsome
face was now lit up yet perplexed. They were prevented from
getting a fair view of the proceedings by the concourse of
older people who had forged forward in front of them.*

*Again the Santa Claus demanded to know whether the
Pembrook children were present, then said, "I have a Christmas present, a very particular handsome piece of business for
Miss Ann Pembrook so she had better come and see Santa by
all manner o'means. It's the grandest present ever I brought
at Christmas at any time whatsoever."*

*At that I again looked towards the children. Ann's brother
straightened himself, took his wee sister by the hand, and
led her forward.*

*I will not burden you, my dear friend, with a detailed ac-
count of what followed. Suffice to say, that the large farm
wagon was positively full to overflowing with gifts which
your dear nephew and your servant Walsh had selected and
purchased for the joy and rehabilitation of this neglected and
destitute family. When I mention the items of three mat-
tresses, complete cooking equipment, winter clothes suitable
for the entire family, toys galore, you will form some idea of
the extent and thoroughness in which this act of mercy was
conceived and consummated.*

*I don't think I exaggerate when I say that there was hardly
a completely dry eye among my forty-odd guests. The ec-
stasy of the three children, the wonderment and gratitude of
the parents, the spirit of Christmas which the event awoke
in all of us must ever remain as a cherished memory.*

*I have made no mention of John. He sat quietly by him-
self on the wagon seat, only now and again whispering some
suggestion to Walsh, who dispensed all of the gifts.*

One must not forget Walsh's part. He carried through with great energy, tact and humor, and kept his formidable audience in a constant ripple of laughter. He was not recognized except by a dozen of those present who were familiar with his odd use of words.

When the last gift had been bestowed, they were all replaced in the wagon, except those belonging to the younger members. Walsh shook hands with the three children, which delighted them beyond measure, climbed up on the wagon, started the six white mules with a great flourish, aroused them to a trot and, with all bells jingling, he and John disappeared.

We then repaired to the house. I introduced the Pembrooks to my other guests, arranged for five extra places at table and we commenced another round of toasts in honor of so happy an occasion.

Just as we were about to start into the dining room John joined us. Nothing would do but that the Sheriff and Major Padget have their way, so we again adjourned to my library and had a glass of punch in which to drink John's good health. Certainly the events of the morning had put us in excellent spirits. My old house, not in its long history ever witnessed such merriment nor such excellent singing.

I had asked Mrs. Pembrook to do me the honor of sitting by me at dinner. Her profile was indeed very lovely. Beauty and breeding are as a cloak for one never could have recalled that she was shod in shoes evidently belonging to her husband.

Major Padget addressed us in his usual gracious manner. Out of consideration for the Pembrooks he did not refer directly to the bounty which had been showered upon them. He did, however, propose a toast to you, expressing how happy a coincidence it was that wealth and opportunity to be bountiful towards others, should be given to those of kindly hearts, and I, my dear friend, will close this far too long letter by expressing my appreciation in that you should have selected this, my home countryside for the distribution of your Yuletide largesse. You have a right to take pride in the manner in which your faithful nephew conducted himself and served you as a faithful steward.

Surely I need not tell you that had I known what was on the boy's mind my complaining letter would never have been written. I also did Walsh an injustice which I regret.

Now that the excitement of Christmas has come and gone I contemplate no trouble in consummating John's horse trade for the boy's heart is set on the little horse he has been hunting. We will collect the money from Mr. Peckett at the bank and close the transaction.

Yours faithfully,
Cavendish Culpepper

Judge Culpepper
to
Colonel Weatherford

My dear Colonel:

I know not how to write this letter nor how to break the distressing and alarming facts which I must needs impart. The money is gone, all of it. The boy procured it from Mr. Peckett. I have indeed managed your affairs in a deplorable manner and offer my fullest apologies.

So considerably shattered am I by this untoward calamity that I know not how to address myself to the boy pending

receipt of your counsels. In my first confusion and aston-
ishment I did say to John, "My dear boy, didn't you want
that fine little horse for Christmas?"

He looked at me steadfastly for a moment, then replied,
"Yes sir, I wanted him more than,—more than, well, I wanted him very much, sir." With that he left me.

I beg of you, my dear Colonel, favor me with your early
advises. If you feel that I should make reparation, pray command me.

Faithfully,
Cavendish Culpepper

Colonel Weatherford
to
Judge Culpepper

My dear Judge:

I have just this moment returned to Millbeck from a
Christmas of fine contentment in Boston and find your two
letters awaiting me. Pray do not distress yourself concerning
John's free choice of action.

Well, bless my soul—six white mules, bells a-tinkling,
red tassles a-waving, whips a-cracking, dogs a-barking,
colored people cheering, a fine family with gladness in their
eyes and relief in their hearts. Join me, my dear old friend, in
saying as did Tiny Tim, "God bless Christmas."

Once as you remember, a certain man went down from
Jerusalem to Jericho and on that road fell among thieves who
robbed and wounded him and left him nigh unto death.

As a matter of fact no one was robbed and wounded and left by the wayside that day. No, my dear Judge. That road down to Jericho was just the road of life. On this we catch a fleeting view of three travellers, travellers much like you and little John and me. Two of them passed by on the other side.

I am well pleased with my nephew. He does my family great honor.

Faithfully and affectionately,
                                        John Weatherford

Mr. Nip and Mr. Tuck

MR. NIP AND MR. TUCK

WHEN I reached the top of Welcome Hill, he and Colonel Weatherford's horse "Laird of Landsdowne" were waiting there watching hounds draw the Willow Beds. They were alone.

His hair was quite white and he wore a black patch over the left eye. He had but one arm. The rein of the snaffle bridle was tucked under his right knee so that he could hold his pipe.

He looked at me, and again turned towards the Willow Beds. I sat down on a chestnut stump and watched all of those big fields that led away from the covert. I have seen the fox cross those fields, oh, ever so many times.

Pretty soon the gentleman, without even turning towards me, said, "So you are having a bit of sport afoot, eh, my boy? You tramped, from wherever you live, to the meet, then tugged up this stiffish bit of a nubbins in the hope of viewing the fox when he broke covert. By Jove, old chap, that's the way. Take your sport where you can, when you can, as you can and enjoy it to the full. You see, under the rules you don't get a second try at the wickets in life. There is only one inning, with never a call to the bat a second time. Get the most out of the old show while your inning lasts. If you want to see a good fox accounted for stick with hounds till the end. Don't get fuddling about in your mind with thoughts of a hot tub, dinner jacket and whiskey and soda. They will await a good sportsman's homecoming."

I told him that I always came to the meet at the Willow
Beds because it was the only one I could reach on foot and
that I couldn't have a pony because my grandfather, with
whom I lived, said that it was only by the help of Mr. Nip
and Mr. Tuck that we squirmed through each month.

"Do you know Mr. Nip and Mr. Tuck, Sir?" I asked him.

He didn't answer for quite a long time but kept looking at
me, then said, "Mr. Nip and Mr. Tuck. Yes, old boy, I have
met them—met them when I was only a year or two older
than you, while sailing a jolly wee bit of a boat in a Scottish
Loch and needed help—met them riding the course at Ain-
tree—pretty ticklish that was for a second at Beecher's
Brook. They stood by me bravely one night at Europe's famous Casino when I asked more of them than a fellow has
any right to ask of anyone. I met them time and time and time
again in South Africa, India, Bagdad, the Sudan, and in our
little 1914 affair with the Germans. Lots of good fellows and
their kith, kin and sweethearts at home were depending on
me just a bit in those days. They are very helpful lads, old
Nip and Tuck."

To hear this made me think of grandfather, so I said,
"Please, sir, I do hope they don't stay away very long at those
places—not when the first of the month comes because what
would grandfather do then?"

"Oh, they will be back," he answered. "They will be back
—devilish efficient, you know, perfect bricks, bred right,
that's the thing—Eton, Trinity, Guard Regiment, top clubs
and all that sort of fuss and feather."

I knew that whatever that gentleman told me would happen, was bound to happen. It had to. It just had to.

Right then my friend Mr. Madden, our huntsman, blew
his horn. The gentleman stood up in his stirrups and looked
and listened. "Covert blank," he said. "Where will hounds
draw now?"

"Highminster," I told him, "then the big woods back of The Black Man's Anvil."

After that he sat so long looking over towards Highminster listening to one hound speaking to what Mr. Madden calls "a start and stop, head and tail, back and forth, hundred-year-old night line" that I thought he had forgotten me. I wanted awfully to talk to him about hunting and lots of things, but Eddie Walsh, Colonel Weatherford's second horseman, had told me that I must never talk when hounds were speaking because real fox-hunters listened so as to be sure where hounds were, and what they were doing and didn't want to hear people talking and talking.

When the hound stopped speaking the gentleman asked me what I was going to be and do when I grew up. I told him there was one thing I had to do before I grew up, and thought I should start pretty soon because it might take a long time. He wanted to know what it was so I told him that my friend, Eddie, had said I should go hunting in Melton-Mowbray in England because it was the most wonderful hunting in the very whole world, so I was going to Melton-Mowbray, only I didn't know which road I should take.

"Melton-Mowbray," he said, sort of to himself, "the old Meltonians. Capital idea! Jolly good place, Melton-Mowbray! You must pop in on me. I'll put you up on a decent sort of nag—a game old chap and if you'll give him his head and leave him alone he'll romp along with the best of the first-flighters. Don't forget to look me up. I live but an hour's hack away."

"Is it a very far walk, sir, to Melton-Mowbray from here?" I asked him.

He refilled his pipe, lit it and smoked while I waited for him to answer. Then he said, "No, it's not far if you want to go there badly enough. No place on this earth is very far to reach, nor any road long to travel for those who have great dreams. The only long road is the road to peace and happiness and contentment and a quiet spirit. It is such a long road for a wee boy like you and so full of twists, turns, blind alleys and false directions, and its roadsides are ablaze with bazaars which have nothing to offer except make-believes, but you will get to Melton-Mowbray some day, old chap, if it means enough to you."

Then he asked me where I was going to live when in Melton-Mowbray so that he would know where to find me. I showed him the picture of the house which Eddie Walsh had cut out of an English magazine for me.

The gentleman read aloud what the magazine said about my house, "26 Masters', 12 servants' bedrooms, 9 baths, ball room, central heating, stabling for 24 horses, stud groom's cottage, 8 car garage, etc., etc."

"Thank you," he said. "I know the place. It's quite comfortable and handy. You can get six days a week hunting from there without too much petrol."

Just then hounds opened in the woods back of The Black Man's Anvil. I knew that the nice gentleman could never, never find the rides and old wood roads that would take him to hounds but I didn't want to go down off Welcome Hill to show him the way. If I did I would never be able to get to hounds or even see them again and would have to just climb all the way up Welcome Hill again and go home.

While I was thinking about this and thinking that perhaps hounds would never meet at the Willow Beds again this whole year, I looked at the black patch over the gentleman's eye and the sleeve cut off up near the shoulder.

"Come on, sir," I cried. "Come on, come on. They have found. He might leave the covert very quickly. I'll show you the way to hounds."

I raced down Welcome Hill and across the Willow Beds meadow as fast as I could. The gentleman came down quite slowly, standing up in his stirrups, listening and looking off to where hounds were working.

There is a big fence at the far side of the Willow Beds into Mr. Benham's oxen pasture. It is a stone wall with four riders on top. An old lane runs along the take-off side of the fence and the rains have washed the earth from the lane so that the fence gets higher and higher each year. Mr. Benham has wired the riders to the stakes and put staples over the wire so you can't get the top rider off. Eddie Walsh says that people make more excuses for not jumping that fence than for not going to church.

When the gentleman saw the fence, he said, "The Meltonians wouldn't fall in love with timber that size. It takes a bit of doing, but ah, there are Mr. Nip and Mr. Tuck up in that hemlock tree so we'll roll on down to it. Here we go." I was very glad indeed that he was on the "Laird of Landsdowne," Colonel Weatherford's best horse.

I wouldn't know how to tell about the way they jumped that fence. The Laird was galloping. He really was and looking at the fence and thinking about it. He has won the Millbeck Cup twice and can jump most awfully fast. The lane is very rough, stones, weeds, and washed-out wagon ruts. The Laird didn't want anything to do with the lane so he took off away, 'way, 'way before he came to it. It was wonderful to see the nice gentleman high over the top of that great fence, sitting up straight in his saddle, not leaning forward like my friend, Eddie Walsh, who is the best rider in the very whole world. When he was still in the air he called out, "This is a bit of all right, eh, what?"

After I had climbed the fence, the gentleman rode back, dropped his rein on the Laird's neck, leaned over, shook hands with me and said, "Thank you for guiding me. It's been jolly and I have enjoyed it. Just hold this precious old thing by the bridle a moment."

He fixed his hat firmly on his head, stood up in his saddle, put the end of the rein under him, got a hold of the rein where he wanted it, pulled the end free, and said, "Thank you, old man. Cheerio. Good luck. I'll be waiting for you at Melton-Mowbray. Commend me to Mr. Nip and Mr. Tuck." He trotted on to the far corner of the pasture where I had told him he would find a lane that would take him to a wood-road near where hounds were pushing their fox out of the covert.

I knew that because I had come down into the valley I would never be able to see any more of that hunt no matter where I went or how far I walked so I climbed back up Welcome Hill. It is long and steep but is the shortest way home. All of a sudden the hills and the fields and the woods seemed big and lonesome and empty and quiet.

At the top of the hill I sat down on the same chestnut stump and took the picture of my house at Melton-Mowbray out of my pocket and started thinking of the 24 horses, how they would look while they were being groomed in the morning, how they would look, back in their boxes. I think red blankets are very pretty.

I wished I had a picture of the Stud Groom's cottage and wondered whether he would have a wife like Mrs. Madden, and whether they would ever say, "Come in for some supper, John David."

After that I did what I said, lots and lots of times I would not do. I started thinking of how much I wanted a pony. I didn't mean to do it and tried not to do it. Anyway I only meant to think about it for a jiffy. But the trouble is, when you get thinking about a pony, you can't stop. Why, as quick as anything, you see what it looks like, and it has a name, and if you don't get right up and run and do something else before you know it you are riding it, then you are out hunting, and you jump a fence, then a bigger fence and you go faster and faster, then you hear Colonel Weatherford say to Mr. Madden, "God bless my soul, Madden, look at John David go. I can't keep up with him." Well, like I said before, you can't stop thinking about a pony for ever so long if you once start and when you do stop, nothing is fun. So I started running towards home as fast as I could and kept saying that I had to clean my bantam house and fix the two places in the wire where my rabbits live.

Late in the afternoon I went up into grandfather's hay loft, opened the door, sat down in the hay and waited to hear the hounds at the kennels make what Mr. Madden calls "a bloody how-do-you-do." That would mean that the Hunt was coming home and was not far away. It grew darker and darker and I thought maybe they had come home without my knowing it because the Hunt had never been so late before. Then I heard the hounds, hurried down the ladder, ran across the fields to the Kennels road and climbed up on a big stone. It was pretty dark, but I saw Mr. Madden coming down the road on his white horse, "The Woldsman," with hounds all around him.

Mr. Madden said, "Hello, John David, it was the run of the year, two hours and fifty minutes. We put him to ground at the north end of Briarcliff—all hounds at the earth except Timely and Vespers and they came to the horn when we were crossing Bethel Uplands. We've been four hours hacking home. Come in for some supper."

Next Colonel Weatherford came riding along on Athelstane, talking to the nice gentleman, then Mrs. Ashley, Miss Sedgwick, Mr. Pendleton, Mr. Newcombe and Mr. Estey. No one else was left of all the people who met at the Willow Beds.

When the nice gentleman saw me he stopped the Laird of Landsdowne and said, "That's right, old chap, that's the proper caper. Stick to the day's sport to the very end. Remember, I'll be waiting for you at Melton-Mowbray. Thank you again for helping me. Cheerio, good luck and God bless you."

It snowed last night. I can see Welcome Hill from my window. It is all white. Maybe the snow has drifted over the stump I sat on when I talked with the nice gentleman, and has filled the gullies in front of the big jump into Mr. Benham's oxen pasture.

I hope the snow doesn't stay, and more and more snow come before Christmas because if it does Colonel Weatherford will say, "God bless me, Madden, we will end the season right now. Let the hounds and horses down."

If there isn't a lot of snow on Christmas, Mrs. Madden will take me to the meet and we will follow the Hunt in Mr. Madden's car. She always invites me on Christmas. Grandfather hasn't any car now.

I found out who the nice gentleman was. The Millbeck paper told about him. Grandfather read it to me. It said, "Colonel Weatherford had as his guest over the week end the distinguished British officer, Field Marshal Lord Actonderry, whose leadership of Empire troops in South Africa, India and the crucial days of 1914–1917 has become legendary. His Lordship was one of the premier Masters of Foxhounds in England." I cut this out and pinned it to the piece of paper which tells about my house at Melton-Mowbray. I think knowing the gentleman's name will make it easier for me to find him when I get to Melton-Mowbray.

Wasn't it nice of a general who was once a Master of Foxhounds to go hunting with me on Welcome Hill all that time and not to care that I didn't have a pony and was only on foot?

While I have been writing this last part I have been thinking about something I'm going to do so I can't write any more —not right away.

From *The Hopewell Junction Gazette*

State Trooper Joe Kelly picked up a small boy at the outskirts of this village on Thursday evening.

The little lad had removed one shoe and was limping along. When asked where he was headed, he replied, 'To Melton-Mowbray in England. A nice gentleman is waiting for me. If I had known how far it was, I would have worn my good shoes. These hurt.'

The boy turned out to be John David Fitzwilliams, grandson of General Trowbridge Fitzwilliams with whom he makes his home at Millbeck. He showed Joe a picture of the house he was going to, invited him to visit him and promised to take him fox-hunting. Officer Kelly motored the wee wanderer back to his grandfather's.

From *The Millbeck Chronicle*

In accordance with an old custom the Millbeck Hunt closed its season on Christmas day and was favored this year with perfect weather and excellent scenting conditions.

Before recording the details of the exceptionally brilliant run of that day, we pause to mention a small ceremony which took place at the Meet.

Just before hounds entered the covert, Colonel Weatherford called The Field together, reminded them that it was Christmas morning and then read the following letter from his recent guest, Field Marshal Lord Actonderry.

Dear Weatherford:

Thank you for sending me the clipping from your local paper about little John David.

The lad made a gallant try. What a crack soldier he would

make—trudging all those long straight, dusty miles at his age—the lonesomeness, doubts, and perplexity as to the way, his sore little feet, darkness coming on yet trudging, trudging, trudging ever forward to Melton-Mowbray to meet me. God bless him.

Do you recall Kipling's poem "Boots"? My father commanded Her Majesty Victoria's regiment of foot which inspired that poem—

"We're foot-slog-slog-slog-sloggin' over Africa,
Foot-foot-foot-foot-sloggin' over Africa,
I-'ave-marched-six-weeks in 'ell an' certify
It-is-not-fire-devils-dark or anything,
But boots-boots-boots-boots-movin' up an' down again."

Weatherford, the formidable number of people now hunting in your American hunting countries does not in itself assure the continuation of the sport. No, my dear old chap, hunting during the black eras will survive only through the devotion and effort of lads like John David. You and I want the sport to carry on.

By the time you receive this, another Christmas will be just around the corner. Buy John David a pony with the enclosed draft—a gay, wee pony that can jump a bit—and be a good fellow and let the pony nibble in one of your paddocks.

May I remind you that He whose day we are about to commemorate reserved a place in his thoughts and heart for all little lads like John David.

Sincerely,
Actonderry

P.S. When you present the pony, just say that it is a Christmas remembrance from Mr. Nip and Mr. Tuck.

Following this, little John David Fitzwilliams, who was sitting in a car with Mrs. Will Madden, some distance off, was sent for.

When the boy had threaded his way through horses and hounds and reached the Colonel, Will Madden blew the call which he employs to announce that the sought for quarry has been found. As the notes of the horn faded among the hills of Highminster, Eddie Walsh appeared leading a diminutive pony, saddled, bridled and with mane and even the upper reaches of the tail meticulously braided.

Colonel Weatherford dismounted, removed his velvet cap, shook the boy by the hand, saying, "Merry Christmas, John David, Merry Christmas.

"This is your pony which Eddie Walsh is going to feed and keep for you. Good hunting, my boy, good hunting, and John David, on the morning you unselfishly ran down Welcome Hill and lost your day's sport, two old friends of yours were standing by wondering what you would decide to do. The pony is a Christmas remembrance from Mr. Nip and Mr. Tuck."

Faith, Perfect Faith

FAITH, PERFECT FAITH
A Christmas Day Fox Hunt

WHEN, in ancient times, the religious significance of Christmas was augmented by the giving and receiving of gifts, and the introduction of our now well-loved Yuletide customs, the festival became in measure dedicated to children.

And so it fittingly came to pass that the fox, a big romping old customer which on Christmas morning we unkenneled and viewed away from the Willow Beds, served the children well.

As against making a far distant point into our stern north country, he ran in pleasant, leisurely circles. Even the youngest child on the smallest, wooliest, ancientest of ponies, saw something of the hunt and felt important and satisfied. Not within memory had Millbeck people, old and young, enjoyed a happier day's sport. In the spirit of the season, the most ardent of the first-flighters forgave the scent for being on the light side.

At the end of one hour and twenty-odd minutes, the fox brought us back to the Willow Beds where he had been found, after having carried hounds into the East, South and West.

But the hour glass was running against many of the field.

For some there were long hacks home with the pace con-
trolled by wee, shoeless ponies, and many turkeys had to be
carved and wish-bones and drumsticks awarded.

Hard decisions were in the making for those to whom
Christmas duty ranked above sport. To pull out from a run
before the fox is accounted for deprives one of the afterglow
—which is the reward for being present. None of us, a child
least of all, ever wants to turn his back to the hunted line.

The fox was not concerned with these human problems.
He was rugged and fit, in no sense blown and now appeared
to be heading into the North for hounds were driving steadily
northwards.

Suddenly the cold, crisp December air resounded with a
cry. "Have at him! Have at him! Hoick forrard! Have at him,
lads!" Will Madden the Huntsman's, ringing, exultant voice.
Hounds had viewed their fox. With triumphant clamor they
were swinging right-handed towards the alders.

My ever sensitive little mare, St. Margaret of Ives—she of
such fond and gallant memories, gave a gentle, challenging
snatch at the bridle. "No, no, old girl," I muttered, "this is
not *our* day." A moment before I had relieved Mary Patterson by undertaking the guardianship of the lead-rein attached to her five-year-old daughter's white pony.

"Now then, Mary," I exhorted, "come on, come on. Boot
the pony with your heels. That's it. That's it. See if you can
get him to trot. Sit tight. Here we go."

"Mr. Pundletoon, why is everybody running away from
us as fast as they can? Where is my Mummy?"

"That's what I'd like to know, Mary. I would like to know
it very much."

"Aren't I going fast, Mr. Pundingleton? Isn't Sugar Puff
running fast?"

"Yes, yes, Mary, you are a noble pair of fox hunters, real
first flighters."

"Oh, there is everybody, Mr. Pundudleton. There is my Mummy. That is the Spring House. I know where I am, Mr. Pundletoon."

A moment later I was leading little Mary by the hand into the Spring House to see her first fox which glared down on us from an old hand-hewn oaken timber.

Above the babble of hounds, horses and men without, I heard Dick Estey say, "Well, Colonel Weatherford, aren't you going to let hounds have him?" and the Colonel's gruff reply, "Kill that fox on Christmas Day? Kill him in front of these children on Christmas? God bless my soul, no, and what's more, I will make sure that no one else kills him."

As the Colonel and I were riding home with Will Madden and the hounds down the long, straight, unbending reaches of the Bagdollen road towards Hopehanesville corners, I fell to thinking of how contented the Colonel had a right to feel that Christmas morning respecting the Millbeck Hunt. He had developed a sterling pack of hounds, recruited a splendid huntsman and staff, mounted them well on rugged blood horses, but best of all, he enjoyed the good will of some three hundred friendly landowners, farmers all.

I had just resolved, in the spirit of Christmas morning, to give expression to these reflections when the Colonel jarred them out of me by saying, "Pendleton, would you happen to know how much of a man's epidermis could be removed and still leave him able to potter about in a mild fashion—picture puzzles and that sort of nonsense?"

I avowed complete ignorance of the matter but asked if anyone of his acquaintance was in such extremes.

"No," he replied, "but a half mile back I fell to thinking about my second horseman, Eddie Walsh, and of how, on this so pleasant day, he had caused, as he has so often done before, the only discordant note."

"You see, Pendleton," he continued, "I gave little Marion

Ashley a pony for Christmas and wanted the child to have a good time out with all the other children this holiday morning. I delegated Walsh to take her hunting. No one in this countryside, not even our huntsman himself, can guide a child through and across the Millbeck country and keep them in such good company with hounds as can Walsh, yet he never even got the child to the Meet nor to any stage of the hunt. I am sorry she should have been disappointed."

The Colonel looped his reins over his left forearm, filled and lit his pipe, dismissed Walsh from his mind and we rode on, chatting contentedly of this and that.

Pursuant to ancient custom, I was to have Christmas dinner with the Colonel and partake of a wild turkey which he had shot and brought home from Hilton Head. Late in the afternoon Enid Ashley and Dr. Sedgwick, our revered old rector, were to drop in for bridge.

When I reached the Colonel's, he put on a show of cordiality, but, through years of companionship, I detected that he was irritated.

As we were pulling up to the fire his man, Albert, informed him that the ever-offending second horseman, Eddie Walsh, had arrived. The Colonel turned to me saying, "Pendleton, a most disagreeable event has happened. The little figure of the infant Christ—a superlative example of early Italian wood carving, has been stolen from our village church. It was to have been used this Christmas afternoon, as always, in connection with the Children's Service. Dr. Sedgwick telephoned and asked me, as Senior Warden, whether I had any suggestions as to what could or should be done towards detecting the thief."

"I have sent for my groom, Eddie Walsh, because, as you know, he is intimate with the more disreputable elements in this part of the county. Also, if you will bear with me, I wish to question him about this morning's performance."

Walsh was sent for and interrogated in exceedingly plain, forceful language as to why he had failed to bring little Marion Ashley to the Meet.

I have rather forgotten the details of Walsh's defense. There was something about having to find and tack a pair of front shoes on the new pony because the pony's feet were tender and the ground hard and rutty. Then I seemed to recall Walsh telling how old General Le Courte's huge, Russian wolf hound, a good natured giant of a dog, had bounded across the lawn towards the pony. In panic, the pony had turned tail and fled down the road; the dog, which was quite as large as the pony, bounding gayly alongside.

Considerable time was lost by these two events and others of a minor note so that the Field had moved off when Marion and Walsh arrived at the Meet.

Respecting the rest of the morning Walsh confessed in his usual frank, forceful, colorful and always sincere manner that he had guessed wrong as to which way hounds would run and just seemed to keep on guessing wrong. He expressed deep regret which I knew full well he must have felt.

That matter being disposed of, the Colonel told Walsh of the happenings at the church. To this very day, years and years later, the tone and the note of disdain in the Colonel's voice echoes on. "Walsh, that theft was a dastardly act—a sneaking, thieving act of an utterly depraved, unfeeling character. We must assume that the statue was stolen for monetary reasons for it was of very substantial value. No man ever stooped lower for money."

The Colonel turned to me, saying, "Pendleton, it is inconceivable that such a crime could have been perpetrated in a village such as ours where we all know each other and respect each other. I am not so much concerned with the statue itself. A Children's Service would be quite as impressive with the manger occupied by a figure lacking such artistic merit, but I purpose apprehending the thief if it is humanly possible."

The Colonel remained silent a moment, glaring straight ahead of him at a portrait of that well-known and notorious sportsman of the past, John Mynton, which hung on his west wall. Suddenly he snapped out, "I never liked that fellow, Mynton. God bless me if I don't think he would have snatched that statue if he had needed money. I will have him taken down tomorrow."

"Walsh," he continued, "if there are any disreputable people in this part of the world you are most certainly acquainted with them. I want you to devote your time, all of it, for a week and see if you can find any clue as to whom the thief may be. Procure such money as you need from my secretary for gas, entertainment, temptation and bribery and do your best. That will be all, Walsh."

Walsh, in spite of a predilection for fighting his cocks at every possible opportunity and being acquainted with the more prominent members of the sporting fraternity between the Bronx and Saratoga, was one of the most impeccable, honorable, upright characters ever to cross my path. He was a staunch member of St. Joseph's Church in Millbeck and took his religion, as he took everything in life, seriously, vigorously and wholeheartedly.

When the Colonel dismissed him he promised to do his very best. This I knew he would do because the sacredness of the object involved would arouse him and he was bound to resent such an act of pillory being committed in his own village of Millbeck.

Upon Walsh's departure, my old friend settled back in his favorite arm-chair, stretched his long legs towards the fire and said, "God bless me, Pendleton, forgive me for interjecting you into such matters on Christmas Day. They are now disposed of. We had a top morning, didn't we, and now a good dinner lies ahead of us. Later on we will take our dogs, yours and mine, all seven of them, for a leisurely stroll, then we'll have a game of cards with two of the most card-minded people in Millbeck. Pendleton, you and I have much to give thanks for this Christmas Day and I do give grateful thanks, and I hope that Clarence Marona, whom I asked to keep an eye on the Spring House until the fox left it, is now home at his dinner."

As I write, I re-live in memory much of the pleasure and contentment of that long ago Christmas dinner, even to the fine, robust 1873 Montrachet White Burgundy.

At my urging, the Colonel recounted the shooting of the Hilton Head turkey—the grey December dawn, the silence, the waiting, the flight of the great bird, the quick, purposeful, effective shot as the turkey appeared against the sky for an instant as it passed between the tops of the pines.

This put us in the mood for reverie and we recalled days of good sport we had spent together from Canada to the Keys of Florida,—upland days; early dawns and quiet twilight hours where the sea meets the land; sultry lagoons; gay, blue, open southern waters; grim northern torrents.

Towards the late afternoon we took our dogs, all seven of them, along the stream which bordered our own properties, the Colonel stumping along in his weather-beaten deer-stalker, blackthorn in hand.

When we returned, dusk had brought the short December day to a close and Enid Ashley and Dr. Sedgwick had just arrived.

At the end of a half or perhaps three-quarters of an hour of bridge the Colonel, being dummy at the moment, was standing in front of the fire. His man Albert entered the room and whispered some message to him. When I looked up, the Colonel was quietly rubbing his hands together and smiling to himself. At the conclusion of the hand he addressed Dr. Sedgwick.

"Sedgwick, my excellent boy, Eddie Walsh, has discovered

the thief and actually recovered the lost figure. I will send for him. We must learn the details. I don't know whether he has captured the wretched knave who did the stealing or not. We will find out."

The Colonel delved into his pocket, took out his old, well worn, pig-skin wallet, explored its contents, extracted a crisp one hundred dollar bill, meticulously folded it, placed it under the ash tray on the card table and sent for Walsh.

The hero of the hour appeared bedecked, in honor of Christmas, in his famous checked waistcoat and carrying his black-and-white checked cap, one of his choicest possessions, in his hand.

"Walsh," said the Colonel, "you have done exceedingly well. I am greatly pleased and Dr. Sedgwick is very grateful. Now then, stand over there where we can hear you. We want all the details. But first tell me, Walsh, is the thief in captivity, or if not, do you know where we can lay our hands on the wretch?" Walsh replied that he knew where the thief was.

"All right," replied the Colonel, "now get on with the story."

"Well, please sir, this morning, just a mite after sun up, while I was doing your Honour's horse, Athelstane, getting him ready for the Hunt, I heared a pattering outside on the gravel, opened the stable door, and it be Miss Marion Ashley on her new pony.

"I tell her that it was a redicaloose thing, by all manner o'means, her, not much more than a baby, being away over to our place at any such hour of a winter morning.

" 'Eddie,' she says, 'I be in the orfulest, turabulest trouble.'

"Course, sir, her and me, if you and Mrs. Ashley will please excuse me, be great friends, so I put the pony in a stall, took Miss Marion in the cookroom, got her a chair, shook up the fire and told her to tell me what all the trouble was about.

"When she was a mite warm and comfortable she says to

me, 'Eddie, every night, every single night, for ever and ever so many nights, I have prayed to Jesus to please let me have a pony.

" 'Well, Eddie,' she goes on, 'one day Miss Sedgwick told me that it was wrong of me to want nice things for myself unless I did nice things for other people, but if I was willing to do nice things for other people, then it might be all right for me to want nice things for myself.'

"Miss Marion then told me, sir, that that night when she was to bed and ready to say her prayers she tried to think of something nice she could do for Jesus, but couldn't think of anything. Then to a sudden she heard Will Madden, away up on the Stick Heap hill back of the kennels, blowing his horn, trying to get some hounds in, what he had lost huntin' that day. She said that hearing Madden's horn made her want to go huntin' more than anything in the whole world. Then, please sir, she got the wonderfulest idea. She figured that if she wanted to go huntin' so much, why Jesus would want to go just as much as her. 'Eddie,' she says, 'after that, whenever I asked Jesus please could I have a pony, I promised to take him on a hunt just as soon as my pony came. Well' she goes on, 'I have my pony now, Eddie.'

"When she gets that far, sir, she just stops and sits there looking at me like she thought everything be settled and fixed up, so I says, 'Well, that be a fine bit o' business, that is, by all manner o' means, but how are you going to do any such thing?' 'Why, Eddie,' she goes on, 'I want you to drive me to the church in a car so that I can get Jesus. When we come back, I will take him on the pony over to Mr. Newcomb's hay barn, right by the Willow Beds, and make him comfortable in the hay. He won't mind that 'cause he was borned in some hay in a stable. We will carry him with us on a wonderful hunt 'cause this is his birthday. That's what we are going to do Eddie.'

"If your Honour, please, I was never took so upside down

afore in my life as by such a orful notion as this. Why, I wouldn't have been surprised none if I had been struck down on the floor for even thinking of such a piece of business.

"I told Miss Marion, plain as I could, that not all the hundreds of million dollars in the Millbeck bank or even a chance to get six pair of new riding breeches, or a horse-shoe stick pin, not even money to get my car fixed, not anything at all, would make me do such a business as take her to the church to do that.

"But if you will excuse me, sir, I won't talk too much. Anyway, sir, I took her to the church. It was open and a lady was setting things to rights, up at the altar, getting them all neat and proper for the Christmas Service. Miss Marion goes in to the vestry and comes out with the Young Gentleman."

I became conscious of some movement in the room. The Colonel was approaching the card table. He halted, glared at Walsh and said, "Walsh, can I possibly understand this situation aright? Am I to believe that you took Mrs. Ashley's daughter, in the dark of early Christmas morning, to Grace Church in my car, using my gasoline, and secretly removed a sacred figure from the church? Is that correct, Walsh?"

"Yes, sir," replied Walsh.

There was an audible sound from Dr. Sedgwick's side of the card table, but when I glanced at him, his face was in complete repose. After a moment or two of oppressive silence, the Colonel's cold voice snapped out. "I have two more questions to ask you, Walsh. Were you delayed in getting to the meet by tacking two front shoes on the pony?" "No, sir," replied Walsh.

"Did General Le Courte's dog frighten the pony and cause delay?" "No, sir," again replied Walsh.

The Colonel walked over to the table, lifted the ash tray, removed the one hundred dollar bill, unfolded it in the same meticulous manner in which he had folded it, replaced it in his wallet, returned to the fireplace and said, "Proceed, Walsh."

But before Walsh could continue, Enid Ashley interrupted by saying, "Eddie, as Marion's mother, I would very much like to feel that whatever more you may have to tell us, will be told without exaggeration."

Walsh squared his shoulders and struggled on.

"Please, sir, when we got back to our stable, Miss Marion put what she called a cape on the Young Gentleman—a new red one. She said she had made it for him all herself. It only had one little button and she was worried 'cause it looked like the cape would blow around if we did much gallopin' or leppin'. I loaned her my gold safety pin what Mr. Estey gave me for catching his horse the day he had the bad fall. Then Miss Marion took the Young Gentleman over to Mr. Newcomb's hay-barn.

"When I got to Mrs. Ashley's, Miss Marion was there, ready to go huntin' and she and me talked about how we were ever going to do what we had in our minds. She told me that nobody must see us. 'Eddie,' she says, "if Colonel Weatherford sees Jesus and me he will say, "God bless my soul, child, well, well, well," or something like that.'

"We rode to the Meet the back way, through 'No Man's Land,' and hid our horses in Mr. Newcomb's hay-barn. Everything was all right with the Young Gentleman, so I went up in the loft and could see your Honour and Will Madden and the hounds waiting at the Willow Beds. Miss Marion had made me take the Young Gentleman up with me 'cause she said he had never seen hounds afore and she wanted him to see them and to see your Honour in your pink coat.

"As soon as you moved off, we mounted, Miss Marion carrying the Young Gentleman. She said to me, 'Eddie, don't you think Jesus looks very nice in his cape? Isn't it a nice little cape? It's scarlet. That's what it is, Eddie. I never made one

before. It took ever and ever so long.' I told her that the
Young Gentleman looked very neat and proper, by all manner o' means.

"Almost right away I heard hounds open and said to myself, 'This is going to be orful for you, Eddie, this is.'

"I had to make up my mind what the fox had made up his
mind to do, and then do the same thing as good as I could. I
figured that if the fox went north it would be redicaloose, by
all manner o' means, for us to try to follow hounds. We
wouldn't ever see or hear anything in that big, open gallopin'
country and would just keep gettin' further and further from
home. Loose horses and ponies would be skylarkin' around
with their tack flappin' and I feelin' like I should catch 'em
and then what would I be goin' to do with 'em the way I
would be fixed.

"As your Honour and Mr. Pendleton know, finally the fox
went west but I lay to go straight south and not follow anybody and try to get down to Peckham's Ridge and hide in
some bushes and wait and listen. I told Miss Marion to boot
the pony along as good as she could and mind what she was
about 'cause we had some rough country to cross in a big
hurry. Off we started south, sir, the pony right on the Woldsman's tail. Course, Miss Marion isn't much bigger than
nothing at all and it's the same with that pony."

At this point Dr. Sedgwick held up his hand as a signal
for Walsh to pause, and said, "Young man, am I to understand that you and Miss Marion purposed leaping the various
objects which came in your way while still carrying the figure
of Christ?"

Walsh's expression was one of worry and concern. "That
were our trouble, sir," he answered. "That were our worstest
trouble. You see, sir, I didn't know anything about that new
pony. 'Course Miss Marion is a good, strong little rider over
a small fence and I lay to take down as many top rails as I

could for her, but I was worried every which way about all those stone walls with the riders topside. I could take the riders off, but a body can't pull down a whole stone wall, not when in any such hurry as we were in.

"And Dr. Sedgwick, sir, if you will excuse me, another bad business was Miss Marion riding with only one hand and holding the Young Gentleman in the other. I was feared she would lose her balance and both of 'em fall off."

Walsh turned again to the Colonel. "We started, sir, like I said, the best we could, but hadn't quite got to the end of the Willow Beds Meadow when we came to that kinda blind dry-ditch. It's a mite broad and a couple o' feet or more deep.

"I see right away that the pony might refuse it or stop, and then jump. It is hard to sit a pony when they jump that way, so I tell Miss Marion to get up all the steam she could and keep the pony right back of the Woldsman."

Walsh again addressed the Rector. "Why, Dr. Sedgwick, please, sir, the pony stood back and leaped for all it was worth and jumped twice as wide as the ditch and Miss Marion set him beautiful. She came up to me, smiling and says, 'Oh, Eddie, wasn't that a jump? Jesus loved it.' 'Well,' I says, 'I'm glad,' and off we started again."

Walsh turned to the Colonel. "When we got to Peckham's Ridge, sir, I was sort of wore out, not with pullin' down rails, that was nothing, but I done a lot of worryin'. When you take the rails off those stone walls, the jumps don't be anything for a horse or even a young colt, but they were powerful broad for any such small pony. We had some hard times but went as straight a line to the Ridge as any fox would take. How Miss Marion ever could be pitched back and forth and high off the saddle and come down with such whacks and still hold on to the Young Gentleman, a body wouldn't know. Twice I had to tell her to straighten his red cape. It were all which way. She said she couldn't help it 'cause she had made it too loose for such high jumpin' and wished she had more pins.

"We wasted a mite of time when we got to the deserted lane into Peckham's. That's where the big, five-foot-three bar-way is, and sir, she even looked like she had riz up with the frost.

"Soon as Miss Marion sees the bar-way, she says, 'Oh, Eddie, Eddie, that's a beauty. That's the one. Here, you take Jesus. I want him to have a great high jump on a big horse going fast. He'll love that, Eddie. Go as fast as you can, then come back and take it down for me. Please go fast, Eddie.'

"Well, sir, I told Miss Marion that by no manner o' means, not at any time altogether had there ever been such a wrong thing as for a groom, mounted on a good horse, to jump a bar-way of that size and that I wouldn't do it and would sooner lose the fox and miss the whole hunt."

The Colonel turned to him. "Did you jump it, Walsh?"

"I did, sir," came the reply.

"Well," rejoined the Colonel, "get on with your report. Get us over that bar-way as quick as possible. Be done with it."

"I will, sir. The Woldsman made a grand leap. It seemed like he stood back from here to the front door. I thought he would crash on to the top of it and kill the both of us. It was all my fault for trying to please Miss Marion by letting him step into such high timber so fast. It was bigger than the one down to Maryland and I went as fast."

The Colonel winced, reached for his glass and said sternly, "God bless me, Walsh, get us away from that lane. Get to the top of Peckham's Ridge as fast as you can."

During the next few minutes Walsh wove us, with rapid strides, in, around and about those sections of the Millbeck terrain traversed by the fox during that Christmas morning run. It seemed as though Jesus, little Marion and Walsh must have hidden behind every clump of bushes, in the lee of every barn and in the very center of countless patches of alders.

They viewed the hunted fox a total of five times and twice turned him, for which offense Walsh expressed deep regret and asked forgiveness. In the end, Walsh's hunting instinct had led him back once more to the gap through which you must pass to enter the Willow Beds from the south.

"We were standing, sir, right in the gap, listening, when I hear hounds away to the south and driving towards us. The fox would be wanting to slip through the gap afore long.

"We had come to the end of our hunt for the little pony was bested. His ears were down. Miss Marion was very tired, too, but I told her to please try and get one more short trot out of the pony 'cause we had to get to the alders, back of the Spring House, and hide afore the hounds and Will Madden and your Honour and all the field reached the meadow.

"We started, and sir, we hadn't gone twenty rods afore I heard a thud. I looked back. The pony had stepped in a woodchuck hole clean up to his forearm and turned over. Miss Marion and the Young Gentleman were both lying on the ground. I got to them as fast as I could. She wasn't hurted, only shaken about. Pretty soon she sat up, looked at the Young Gentleman, then on a sudden takes hold of my arm, starts crying in a way I never saw a body cry afore, not out loud—no sound, but crying so hard she couldn't breathe and tears all over her face. She put her head on my shoulder and says, 'Oh, Eddie, Jesus and me had a orful fall and oh, Eddie, look, look, Jesus has broken his leg.'

"Now sir, please, I was in great trouble. Miss Marion said she wouldn't get up—didn't care who saw her now, and wished she could die quick, and it was the same with me. I would have put her up on the pony only she was so sort of soft and limpish she would have rolled right off. Hounds were so close I could hear old Woldsman's voice. I didn't

know what to do. Maybe your Honour would think I should-
n't have done what I did, but anyway I says right out loud,
'Jesus, if you could think of any way to help me out of this,
I would be obliged.' Then just when things were the worst,
if Miss Marion doesn't stop crying, wipe her eyes on her
sleeve, start smiling, then pretty near go to laughing, and
says to me, 'Why, Eddie, it doesn't matter about Jesus. It
doesn't matter the tiniest bit. I forgot that he could fix his leg
anytime he wants to. He has done lots and lots of more wonderful things than that, only he doesn't want to fix it now
'cause he is too 'cited about the hunt. We better hurry, Eddie,
'cause he wants to see everything.'

"She wrapped the broken part in her silk scarf. I put her
up, handed her the Young Gentleman and we went as fast
as we could down to the alders.

"We saw the fox come through the gap and into the meadow. He stopped, listened and looked around.

"An old rabbit hound was tonguing down near us in the
alders to the east. Mr. Alexander and his children were in the
field to the west where the fox had first gone away. From the
south the fox heard the Millbeck hounds driving on towards
him. He started towards the north tip of the meadow but
afore he got there some rabbit hunters fired at a rabbit and
called out to each other. The fox stopped again and looked
around. There was no way he could go where he would not
run head on into people or hounds, so he hid in the Spring
House.

"When the hounds rushed in after him, Miss Marion was
took pertickler bad. She shut her eyes, grabbed hold of my
arm and kept asking, 'Oh, Eddie, Eddie, Eddie, will they kill
our fox?' Then to a sudden she says, 'Oh, Jesus, please,
please, please don't let them hurt him.'

"Right then your Honour and Will Madden galloped up
and brought hounds out of the Spring House. I told Miss

Marion that I couldn't be sure whether hounds had killed the fox or not. She said, 'Eddie, they haven't killed him or hurt him or even frightened him and when everybody has gone away Jesus and you and me are going in to the Spring House to see him.'

"In a little while the field and the hounds went home so we rode over to the Spring House. Clarence Marona was off in some bushes on guard so that no one would bother the fox. He held our horses while we went in to the Spring House. Miss Marion looked at the fox up on the rafter a long time, then said, 'That was nice of Jesus, wasn't it, Eddie?'

"Clarence wanted to get home for his Christmas dinner but didn't know how long it would be before the fox would leave the Spring House. I told Clarence that if he would give me a leg up to the beam and would take Miss Marion and the horses away so the fox wouldn't see them, I would try to get the fox off the beam.

"The fox didn't take to me much when I sat down beside him, but we got on pretty good and both of us scrambled down without getting hurt. I am sorry, sir, that I brought Miss Marion home so late for her dinner, but the pony came on a mite slow.

"After your Honour talked to me this noon I went over to see Miss Marion and told her that you wanted the Young Gentleman taken right back to the church. I have him, sir, in the hall. The little part is tied up in Miss Marion's scarf."

An oppressive and continuing sort of a silence fell upon the room. Finally Enid Ashley walked over and stood with her back to us, looking at a portrait of the Colonel which the members of the Hunt had commissioned Frank Voss to paint. The Colonel is depicted on his favorite old mount, Athelstane, and two famous Millbeck dog hounds, Woodsman and Craftsman, are standing in the foreground. The artist se-lected the Willow Beds meadow because of the views of great stretches of grass lands rising from it as typical of the Mill-beck country. That was the field in which Marion had her fall.

Enid's getting up aroused the Colonel. He took out his wallet, extracted the same hundred dollar bill, folded it as before, called Walsh to him, handed him the bill, saying, "Thank you, Walsh. That will be all. Good night."

Old Dr. Sedgwick was sitting gazing at the fire, but probably not seeing it. There was the semblance of a smile on his wrinkled face. Then he said, more, I think, to himself than to us, "Many ask and receive, but how few, how very few of us try to repay."

"Childhood—lest ye become like unto one of these, ye cannot inherit the Kingdom of Heaven. Faith, perfect Faith."

Mr. Henry P. Throckmorton

MR. HENRY P. THROCKMORTON

The Rev. T. Souther Sedgwick
to
Colonel John Weatherford, M.F.H.

Dear Weatherford:
 I have accepted the Chairmanship of a committee to organize a so-called White Elephant Auction. The proceeds will go towards the purchase of a Hook and Ladder for our splendid Millbeck Volunteer Fire Brigade.
 Consistent with tradition, this equipment is to be gay in color and embellished with many handsome brass trimmings. There is expectation that our friends and neighbors will derive exultation from putting the vehicle through its paces.
 May I count on you to consign some item or items to this worthy venture?
 You are reminded that time, in its passing, is the father of White Elephants. A perambulator, for instance. Ah, my dear Colonel, how such inanimate objects lose their significance.

Cordially,
T. Souther Sedgwick

Colonel Weatherford
to
Dr. Sedgwick

Dear Sedgwick:
I wish you success with your auction. My household will give full support.

The ordering of my life has not exposed me to the acquisition, or employment of a perambulator.

But, my dear Sedgwick, were I the owner of such a lugubrious affair you have my every assurance that it would, by all means, find a place in your sale.

A perambulator! God bless my soul.

> *Sincerely,*
> *John Weatherford*

P.S. Since writing the above I have determined, but, mark you, with some pangs of regret, to consign Henry P. Throckmorton to your auction.

Dr. Sedgwick
to
Colonel Weatherford

Dear Weatherford:
Whereas your cooperation is appreciated, yet I could but wish that it might have been demonstrated in a manner other than through the severance of your ties and companionship with Mr. Throckmorton.

Your friends, all of them, feel that the association has been lively and exhilarating for you both.

True, it is rumored that you have been sorely tried but you are not given to early discouragement.

How often shall I suffer my friend to abuse me? Seven times seven? Nay, seventy times seven.

If you insist on the severance, may I issue a friendly note of warning? Are you quite sure that you should dispose of Throckmorton without giving due notice of his characteristics? Might these not prove confounding and possibly costly to a buyer?

We have no assurance that he will show the same loyalty, affection and companionship to others as he has so handsomely shown to you.

To set my own mind at rest, would you consent to pen a few lines pertaining to Throckmorton which the auctioneer could refer to or read from, and later deliver to the purchaser?

I question whether Caveat Emptor would apply in the case of Throckmorton.

Sincerely,
T. Souther Sedgwick

Colonel Weatherford
to
Dr. Sedgwick

Dear Sedgwick:
The biographical notes suggested by you are enclosed herewith.

J. W.

Biographical Notes
on
HENRY P. THROCKMORTON OF GROTON
by his Associate
John Fortescue Weatherford, M.F.H., Esq., of Millbeck

Some time ago a gentleman of Groton, Massachusetts, whose avocation is developing breeds of prime eating fowl, presented me with 26 day-old chicks.

The letter accompanying this gift contained the following injunction: "Keep a very sharp lookout for Henry P. Throckmorton. He will be readily discernible from the others in a week's time.

"There are but two of this breed in existence for his father was among the last of that famous of all breeds of Irish game cocks, known the world over as the Kilkenneys of Kilkenney.

"His mother, of the Jersey Giant breed, was named 'Giantess St. Agatha of Far Hills,' winner of the Newbald Statuesque Plate awarded at Madison Square Garden to the largest fowl in the exhibition."

The receipt of this gift necessitated my purchasing one of the newly invented "Broiler Compartment Hotels" in which the residents go down as they grow up.

No maternal supervision is provided in these contrivances. Science demands that those in residence be not diverted from eating and drinking by motherly adulation or scolding. One cycle of gorging and drinking follows fast upon the heels of another.

On the third day following the arrival of the chicks, they being then five days old, I took my way to their apartment. It was early in the morning and the attendant, Clan Clancy, had not as yet made his rounds. The water in the drinking trough was low, and the residents, all but one, were huddled close to the trough, uttering plaintive appeals. They could not reach the water with their bills.

The one chick was eating dry mash from the feed hopper. Upon finishing his breakfast, he shouldered his way in ruthless fashion through the dense mass of his compatriots, hurled himself sideways against the grating which was designed to prevent the very artifice he was now attempting, lowered himself down by wriggling, contacted the water, drank, wriggled himself out of the trough, shook himself, again charged through his thirsty fellows, leaving a half dozen of them off balance, and started at once upon his second cycle of gorging. I had met Mr. Throckmorton.

I called again the morning following. Seemingly it takes an attendant or janitor some time to learn how to service a chicken apartment properly. If the hoppers are kept too full, much feed is wasted through spilling; if not full enough, very young chicks cannot reach the food. This was the situation on my second visit.

The chicks were crowding, pushing and chirping in their hunger and apparently persuaded that if they could but gain the position occupied by their neighbors, all would be well.

None were feeding or could feed—that is, none except one. In the center of the line, in the very vortex of the confusion, oblivious of, and indifferent to everything but his own hearty breakfast, was Henry P. Throckmorton, gobbling mash.

He was not appreciably larger than his compatriots nor, at five or six days of age, different in conformation. What, thought I, is his technique? So dense was the mass of chickens around him that I could not at once determine.

By inserting one of my fingers through the grating at Mr. Throckmorton's right and another at his left and gently pushing his immediate neighbors to one side, I observed that

he was standing on the prostrate form of one of his compatriots. That he had consummated this satisfactory arrange-
ment, by means other than gentle persuasion, was quite
evident. Through standing practically on his head, he
was breakfasting, if not conveniently, certainly fulsomely.
Clancy arrived and filled the hoppers.

That day I left for a protracted stay abroad. One of my
first acts upon returning was to betake me for a visit to Mr.
Throckmorton. The chickens had been divided and moved
into the lower apartments. Mr. Throckmorton was not in
residence with them, so I sent for Clan Clancy to make
inquiries.

It is next to impossible to glean specific facts from Clancy
or any other Irishman of his temperament. There is naught
an employer can do other than try to piece together a long
series of dark, veiled, mysterious vagaries and thus arrive at
the approximate truth.

"Ah," said Clancy, "it's very joyful, he is, all the time. A
fine figure of a burrd. Very joyful indeed. It was the wire
mesh, what was in it—the wire mesh what he stood on.
That's what was in it."

Of the minor irritations which assail mankind during a
day's work, few are more irritating than to have a narrator
from whom one is trying to prod the truth, pause, wrap himself up in his own meditations and look dreamingly off to
the far horizon.

With an opponent such as Clancy, one has no alternative
other than to wait.

The mist finally cleared from his eyes. I felt encouraged.
"Ah, thim grand Irish burrds," said Clancy. "Me sister, the
Saints keep a soft eye on her, married a lad from Kilkenney.
She did so. Very joyful he was of a Saturday night.

"Sure, it didn't pleasure your Honour's fine rooster to
stand on the wire mesh. Ah, the big heathen; a wee soft

burrd, patted down like an old bit o' rug, was very agreeable in the night time. It was. He made eight o' thim little rugs. He is a gay lad. He is so."

I counted the remaining seventeen chickens and told Clancy to bring Mr. Throckmorton to me.

A few minutes later the blatant, complaining squeak of an over-loaded wheelbarrow brought me to the door of the wood shed.

Clancy, with extreme effort, was trundling a large oak cage, the front of which was constructed of three-quarter inch iron bars. I recalled that my groom, Eddie Walsh, had purchased the cage years ago at a sheriff's sale in Poughkeepsie, following the collapse of an itinerant circus.

Within the cage reposed the now unbelievably large, stately and emblazoned figure of Henry P. Throckmorton.

"A joyful burrd," said Clancy.

"Release him," I said.

Clancy approached the door of the cage, hesitated, asked to be excused for a moment, retired to a neighboring shed, and re-appeared with a broom in one hand a half bushel basket in the other—an apple picking basket with a handle.

He walked to the cage with faltering steps, leaned the broom against it, put his left arm through the handle of the basket, and poised the basket, chin high, in the manner in which knights of old held their shields. With a deft motion he opened the cage, grabbed the broom and stepped back.

Mr. Throckmorton strode out of the cage, spread his powerful shanks, rose to his greatest height, and glared at Clancy and at me. I lack words to convey a fair picture of his size and strength.

Clancy was moving his right hand up and down the broom handle, getting the feel of it. Evidently there was one spot which would produce the much cherished Irish tingle. Clancy found it, spat on his hand and grasped the broom.

Mr. Throckmorton took a step towards Clancy who elevated his shield nearer his face, gave the broom a quick, circular flourish and called out, "Have a care now, your Honour. Mind your head when he'll be driving you back. Mind the rafters."

Mr. Throckmorton inclined his head to the left and studied Clancy. The basket, serving as a shield, was old and contained a fair size hole in the bottom. Through this I could plainly see parts of Clancy's red, unshaven Irish visage.

"Guard yourself, sir," he said, "and don't be at the back end of him when he scrutches. Ah, he's a grand scrutcher. He'll smother you all together. You'll get no air to breathe while he's at it. He'll take a scrutch afore he tares the garments off us. There he starts. God presarve us, he'll uproot the shed down atop us."

It is only fair to Clancy to record that there was some justification for his warning. When Mr. Throckmorton scratched, the ceiling, up to the very ridge, resounded with the sharp impact of bits of gravel, chips of wood and particles of hard earth.

"Mind now," roared Clancy above the din, "what goes up will come down. It will so. He is in fine joy. Indeed yes."

Mr. Throckmorton took another determined, purposeful step towards Clancy. No pair of shoulders were ever more set and squared away than Throckmorton's. Clancy put his mouth to the hole in his shield, and in a now resigned voice, announced, "If I had known what sport it was your Honour had a mind to play at this day for a nice little diversion, I would have put on me old pants. Indeed yes."

It was time for me to take action. Definitely there was very bad feeling between Clancy and Throckmorton and there was too much game-cock blood in a bird of such unprecedented size and power. I told Clancy to return to his farm operations.

When Mr. Throckmorton and I were at last alone, I procured a handful of grain, proffered it to him in small modicums, constantly lowering my hand. The last of the grain he took companionably.

After so long an absence from home, I had set the morning aside for an inspection of my property and possessions. To my surprise Mr. Throckmorton accompanied me, very erect, dignified, imposing and intensely interested in his first view of the outside world. At the end of an hour, we were still strolling side by side.

I now record that I found in him a delightful companion. He was entirely articulate and, like those who are experiencing new sights and sensations, was fresh and spontaneous.

Possessed as he is of a repertoire of some dozen or more clucks of varying volume and tone, I soon knew what his reactions were to such objects and events as one would witness or encounter on a country property during a morning's stroll.

We paused to observe a brood mare and her three months old foal. This was Mr. Throckmorton's introduction to horses. He was amazed and uttered the sharp, low cluck, indicating that I should keep my wits about me. Suddenly, without warning, the foal whinnied, bounced a foot off the ground and, foal fashion, encircled its mother in reckless abandon. Mr. Throckmorton, who had not associated so formidable an institution with mobility, was taken aback and uttered the cluck indicating "Extreme danger at hand. Everyone for himself."

Having fulfilled his obligation to me, in lieu of a group of matrons, he strode resolutely forward, intending to hurl himself into the innermost center of the melee. He had been astounded at the great size of the mare and foal but certainly not daunted.

He tried to get under the paddock fence, then between the

boards but could not so undertook to fly over the top. He had never before taken to the air and collided with the boards with scrunching force.

Before he could try again the foal settled down to graze beside its mother. Mr. Throckmorton uttered the all clear signal, a soft, soothing cluck and we proceeded on our walk. He turned once to gaze ruefully at the gaudy pattern which his feathers, shed in his contacts with the fence, made on the greensward.

Just before we rounded a corner which would close the paddock from our view, he halted for one last look at the mare and foal. His attitude and expression told as plain as human words could set forth what was on his mind. "Those were hellish big 'what-do-you-call-ems.' Perhaps we are well out of that situation."

At sight of the rose garden he broke into his rolling, uncertain lurch, and upon reaching the soft, rich, damp earth, spread his legs, took the stance of a golfer and prepared to scratch. The garden is protected on the north by a low potting shed. A few feet beyond this the glass of the greenhouse rises above the shed.

Upon being satisfied that his stance was correct, Mr. Throckmorton scratched. I now record that so astounding is his vigor that particles of earth were hurled against the side of the shed, twelve paces distant. Upon hearing the clatter my companion turned, viewed the shed and gave a medium crow. He was about to turn away from what to me appeared a most worthy feat when he noticed the glass of the greenhouse. It stands some twenty feet beyond the shed.

To what fine heights does a challenge exalt a sportsman, or adventurer or man of strength; a fox-hunter at the end of a long run assaying a formidable fence on a tired, or green horse to see the fox accounted for; the yachtsman, half a gale in the offing, increasing his vigilance but declining to reef;

men of exploration ever pressing forward, the quest more important than food or safety; the man of strength ennobled by his effort to outdo his former achievement.

Mr. Throckmorton selected a site for his new effort. He lifted one mammoth, yellow foot high in the air, placed it on the site with nicety of judgment, did the same with the other foot, bent to his task and scratched. Our interests were akin. Would the shrapnel or earth and pebbles, as it rose in fan-like formation, surmount the potting shed and spatter on the glass? It did. The sound was fair music to our ears. "Hurrah!" I called out. "Hurrah! Hurrah! Well done, Throckmorton."

Mr. Throckmorton stood a moment, head on one side, gazing at the goal of his success. He then turned, strode importantly to the driveway, squared his shoulders, crowed, and we walked on.

After a few paces I was conscious that he had veered over closer to me than usual. He uttered six clucks, quite conversational in character. Of course it is anyone's guess as to what he was trying to convey, by practically rubbing knees with me and whispering. It will, however, be conceded that I am in as good a position as the next to interpret the matter and I hold that he said, "Cluck (not) Cluck (so) Cluck (d—d) Cluck (bad) Cluck (eh what?)"

We came at last to my residence and I decided to leave Mr. Throckmorton to his own resources. I mounted the terrace, he mounting beside me. Before closing the door, I glanced back at him. We had companioned each other for the better part of a morning and I was closing the door in his face. He stood perplexed. The old arrogance, his armor against the world, had dropped from him. A tinge of melancholy took its place.

He kept his eye glued upon the door for a long time, now and again uttering low, but sharp clucks, then turned, moved to the edge of the terrace, sat down to rest and viewed my property with evident approval.

The wren, which is nesting in a blue china birdhouse suspended from the eaves by a copper wire, alighted on the driveway. Mr. Throckmorton arose, uttered a sharp note of disapproval and warning and sat down again. I felt that my house was well protected.

Later in the day Mr. Throckmorton took up his residence in the lower branches of an Austrian pine tree which stands a few feet from my bedroom window. To this cozy, protected haven he returns each evening, wearied by the day's labors and adventures.

We have now companioned each other for a long time and I have enjoyed the association and been touched by evidences of Throckmorton's concern for me.

The reasons for severing these ties will perhaps be made understandable in the following record covering but a few of my associate's activities.

THE AFFAIR CUB-HUNTING

One morning I arranged with the Huntsman to take four couple of old hounds and a handful of puppies to Tower Hill for some hunting experience.

I hacked to the Kennels and upon passing the Huntsman's house one of his children burst out laughing. Looking back' I saw Mr. Throckmorton lumbering along behind me.

The efforts of five agile men, three children and a miscellaneous assortment of dogs failing to capture my companion, we left him sitting on the eaves of the kennel's maternity ward and proceeded to Tower Hill.

The dew lay heavy and the old hounds soon had a fox on its feet. He set his mask for Butts Hollow, ran a short mile and then made a series of twists and turns, each bringing him closer to where he had been unkenneled.

Assuming that the fox was working back towards an earth on the west slope of the mountain, I turned my horse's head into the west and a moment or two later entered a clearing on a height of land which overlooks both the Berkshire Hills and the Catskills. I had permitted myself the highly irregular luxury of being between the hounds and their quarry.

Suddenly the early morning stillness was assaulted by a scream of a weirdness difficult to describe. I booted my horse into a canter. A moment later he shied, violently. The ground was strewn with feathers—the gorgeous red, black and blue armor of poor Henry P. Throckmorton. The fox had been that way.

An hour before I had been filled with resentment towards Throckmorton. What my inner feelings were as I looked down on that little pile of disheveled finery are personal to myself.

I will record, however, that my feelings deepened with the realization that as poor, clumsy, stumbling a traveler as he was, my gallant friend had followed me through a rough, briary, tangled terrain and would have pursued his quest to the last that in him lay.

Before I realized it, I was in the midst of the ever-pressing hounds. They forged past me, took a fleeting glance at the feathers and were gone. I turned my old horse, Athelstane, and walked slowly after them. A little later I heard hounds at the earth and Will Madden's ever-stirring cry of Victory for his pack. I turned towards the earth.

While still some ways off, I could see the Whip down on one knee examining the ground. Will Madden was leaning over him.

Hearing me coming, Madden picked up something and walked towards me. "Look, sir," he said, "I have never seen the like of this afore. An eagle must have struck our fox just as he got close to the earth. Look at this hair, sir. It's off the fox's back."

As I looked Mr. Throckmorton crowed from a nearby pine tree.

THE AFFAIR HENRY NEWCOMBE

Some weeks ago I missed a day's hunting through having obligated myself to be in New York.

Upon my return, the following letter from my valued friend and neighbor, Henry Newcombe, awaited me.

Dear Weatherford:

I address myself to you in the manner following, confident that it will be received in good part.

Whereas I write without bitterness, yet I am offended and indignant and, as a resident of this countryside, resolved that appropriate steps be taken to rid Millbeck of what I consider a blight and a pest, namely Henry P. Throckmorton.

I trust you will read this letter seriously and take appropriate steps to dispose of the wretch and so bring comfort and relief to your many friends.

I will now relate a most dastardly affair.

At about 10:15 yesterday morning hounds unkenneled a splendid fox in the swale north of the Black Man's Anvil—a really fine romping fellow.

Ten minutes later as my good horse Swynford's Abbot and I were boiling along by ourselves, a field to the east of the line, the poor fellow went into a hole and we turned over in proper fashion—a really devastating crash. We were both a bit dazed and content for the moment to relax our concern for the hunt.

When I finally started to rise, I heard a whirling sound back of me and Henry P. Throckmorton shot by half running, half flying, charging upon my horse.

My good English Locke hunting derby, a particularly comfortable and satisfying one, lay in your rooster's course. By God, Weatherford, if he did not snatch it up in that tremendous beak of his and continue his charge upon my horse.

Knowing that no clean bred horse could be indifferent to such an intemperate assault, I made haste to reach him. I was too late. Swynford's Abbot, your rooster and my hat were careening down the gentle slope to Thatcher's Brook.

Whereas I was filled with rage and bitter with disappointment at losing what had all the makings of a brilliant run, I could but be diverted by the splendid bravado with which this incongruous pair charged so formidable a brook. They flew it, my horse in his stride, your rooster on the wing.

When they took off, the brim of my hat appeared to be side by side with the throatlatch of the Abbot's bridle. When they landed the horse had gained some three feet. "Well done, well done, old man," I found myself shouting. They disappeared from view.

I was growing stiff, sore and chilled but, reluctant to abandon so good a horse and so comfortable a hat, hobbled along in the hope Throckmorton might discard his trophy. I could find no trace of the horse or hat. My boots had become tight, a button was pressing on my shin bone, my aches grew apace so I made my way towards Thatcher's to telephone for a car.

When close to the house I heard hounds and turned to look eastward. They were running to the southeast and there, galloping towards me, wide open, and I mean wide open, was your always amazing boy Eddie Walsh leading the Abbot full tilt across Thatcher's seventy-acre upland.

He pulled up in front of me, and in a jiffy was off his horse, had my stirrups pulled down, was holding the Abbot ready

*for me to mount, and was saying, his voice vibrant with in-
tense excitement, "Now then, Mr. Newcombe, look smart,
sir, look smart, sir. Up you get, hounds are flying, they are
working up on him, a grand fox by all manner o' means. We
be right where we belong but got to go wide open for a spell.
Here we go, sir."*

*Weatherford, we did go wide open and across a beautiful
bit of galloping country. Walsh may be an unconventional
guide, but he is master of the art. I had a tumultuous and fast
frisk for a mile and a half, and then to my shame found myself ensconced in a locust grove, hiding like a thief and waiting, if you will believe me, for hounds and fox to catch up
with us.*

*Peering out from the fringe of the locusts we saw the fox
speed by us, neck extended, his great grey-tipped brush
sweeping on behind. Hounds were just a small field back of
him, were pressing him and running with tremendous head
and cry.*

*Your fellow Walsh is a born fox hunter. His face was
twitching and his hands and shoulders in constant motion.
He kept muttering to himself, "Drive him, lads, drive him,
drive him." Then he asked me in a voice shaking with emo-
tion if I could see the Huntsman. I told him no. "That's good,
sir," he said. "That's good 'cause I aim to cheer hounds on
when they come." They came. "Have at him, lads! Have at
him," called Walsh. Then, losing all fear of Madden and
knowing that you were not out, he moved to the very edge of
the locusts, stood up in his stirrups and, in a voice you could
have heard in Sharon, screamed, "Hoick, hoick, hoick forward, have at him. Come on, Mr. Newcombe. We have 'em
alone, sir. Sit down and ride for it. They be boiling. The scent
is stinging their noses. I got my knife handy. I'll have his
brush on your bridle in a jiffy."*

*Well, my dear Weatherford, on we went. Madden and the
small field, eight or ten, were three fields back as they had*

been forced to detour around wire, and the pace was such that it was impossible to make up lost ground. Walsh and I had it to ourselves for about three miles till the fox went to ground on the hillside north of the Willow Beds.

Confound it, I started out to give you a piece of my mind about that infernal rooster of yours. I seem to have got off the track, but will come over to see you.

Sincerely,
Henry Newcombe

P.S. After the run I became detached from Walsh and the field and rode on home alone.

A half mile north of the school at Hopehanesville I came upon a small boy playing at knight errantry. He was wielding a piece of a broken fence rail as his weapon and defending his diminutive sister from some imaginary villain. For protection he was relying upon his visor. It was my hat, and d— it, Weatherford, he had punched two eye holes in it.

H. N.

THE AFFAIR EPHRIHAM THE GANDER

As I write this, Mr. Throckmorton is in residence at Dr. Shaw's Hospital for a check-up and undergoing certain repairs, the need of which will be touched upon herein.

Mrs. Wilbur Thompson recently favored me with the following letter:

Colonel Weatherford
Dear Sir:
Eddie Walsh bringed me your letter so I now send bill. It is like this.

My gander, Ephriham what weighed 11 pounds when Mr. Throckmorton done him in, $6.40,

My broom, broke when I tried to clout Mr. Throckmorton, $1.40,

My straw hat, $2.75. It fell off when Mr. Throckmorton was chasing me to the house after he had finished Ephriham. He hid the hat some place, but I can't find it.

About 3 quarts green paint, $2.75, knocked off shelf and spilled on garage floor when Mr. Throckmorton was chasing Ephriham to the top of our car. I couldn't scoop up paint 'cause it went down the drain in garage floor what was too bad.

About my apron. Mr. Throckmorton gave it a yank what most upsetted me. It was kinda old anyway, and pretty well wore out, but it was all wore out when he was finished with it. Maybe you would think 15 cents would be all right.

Col. Weatherford, I feel mostly bad about the wooly toy lamb Mrs. Hugh Collins gave my granddaughter, Maria. It made a baa-baa noise if you squeezed it.

Well, Mr. Throckmorton seemed to feel right frisky when he had finished doing my poor Ephriham in. He saw the lamb, picked it up in his beak and banged it on the ground and it baaed. This sort of pleasured him and now there don't be anything but some little pieces of wool and a half head, but no eye to it.

Do you think Maria could have a new lamb?

Mrs. Wilbur Thompson

WALSH'S REPORT TO ME

Please, sir, I rid over like you said and gave the check to Mrs. Thompson.

Just after I started home, I says to myself, "What happened to Ephriham?" So I rid back and said to Mrs. Thompson, "And where would Ephriham be and how is it that my boss has to pay for him and you keep him?"

She says to me, "Eddie, I didn't keep him. I couldn't. Mr. Throckmorton took him home."

Well, please sir, I figured to myself that there don't be any rooster in the world can carry or drag a gander that size, it be rediciloose, Mrs. Thompson don't be tellin' the truth, so I says, "Which way did he go?" "Back of the garage," she tells me, "and kitty cornered across the little field where we had the corn. I watched him out of the window. It took him till noon to get across the field. He walked backwards pullin' poor Ephriham after him, and had to stop about every fifty feet and rest and get a new hold. He had Ephriham by the neck."

Well sir, I rid across the field and seen feathers all the way. There is a locked gate in the wire fence into Ted Wookley's farm so I couldn't go any further, but could see that Mr. Throckmorton was headin' as straight for our place as a body could draw a line. If you wouldn't mind me sayin' it sir, I think he is bringin' Ephriham home to you sir, as a present.

"That will be all, Walsh. We will not refer to the matter again," I said.

ON THE NINTH DAY THEREAFTER

This morning, shortly before luncheon, my butler informed me that Walsh was in the front hall and wished to speak with me, and, as Saunders put it, "he seems just a bit fluffed up sir, if I might mention it."

When I reached the hall Walsh was holding the door open and indulging in the foible of twitching his neck, which he does when over-tense. I have learned to associate this neck twisting business with something unpleasant about to happen to me.

Walsh said, his voice ashake, "Here they come, sir. Here they come right across the lawn, straight towards the house, if you would have a mind to look, sir." I looked. "Remove it. Dispose of it promptly," I said.

Walsh stood twisting his cap around, thoroughly dejected and cast down. Presently he said, "Please sir, if you would excuse me, it be close to three miles from Mrs. Thompson's place to ours. He has been nine days apullin' and tuggin' at that big gander, up hill and down, across two streams, one of 'em has quick water, then through Mr. Andrew Haight's big swamp, under or around a lot of stone walls, post and rail and wire fences. He been leavin' home at sun up and gettin' back night-time and worried when he was away lest a fox walk off with Ephriham. He brought it all this way for you, sir, so maybe you would have a mind to take a look, just a quick little look, sir, at Ephriham and then say something pleasant to Throckmorton. He had a hard stiff fight gettin' Ephriham for you in the beginnin'."

Down through the years I have constantly exposed myself to anger, irritation and sometimes humiliation through the employment of Walsh and entertain no doubt but that I shall so continue, my life long.

As I sit here in my library and recall that two days ago at about this hour, I walked down my terrace steps, across my lawn in company with Walsh for the express purpose of viewing what I did view, I stand confounded.

I will, however, complete recording this lugubrious event.

When Throckmorton saw me, he came lurching at top speed. He was indeed hollow-eyed, frayed, bedraggled and emaciated, but dynamic as always.

In respect to that which had been Ephriham, I elect to make no comment nor attempt a description.

It must have occurred to Walsh that I was disappointing Throckmorton by not showing more enthusiasm, for Walsh, standing nearer to my gift than it pleased me to approach, proceeded to clap his hands, cheer and wave his cap in the air. Of course any noise or form of motion is easier for Throckmorton to comprehend than are words.

I am anxious to bring this writing to the earliest possible close, so will only add that I, John Fortescue Weatherford, of respectable New England descent, on a gay, beautiful morning, might have been seen standing on my lawn, my hat aloft in one hand, my cane in the other, both in circular motion, while I sang out over the sad remains of a poor woman's tenderly fostered gander, "Well done, well done, Throckmorton." At which Throckmorton stood up on his toes, flapped his wings and crowed.

It is to such depths of ignominy that characters such as Walsh and Throckmorton can at times bring one.

After luncheon I saw Walsh operating the tree-spraying equipment which he had filled with some form of deodorant of his own concoction, preparatory to picking up and removing the late Ephriham Thompson.

THE AFFAIR AUCTION SALE

As a slight gesture of neighborliness to my friend Arthur Pendleton, I recently attended the annual auction of Dutchess County Aberdeen-Angus cattle.

Pendleton and many of my friends have done knowledgable and constructive work in making ours one of the premier counties of the eastern states in the breeding of this stalwart cattle.

Other interests have precluded my taking a part in this enterprise. Nevertheless I bow to the sound achievements of my neighbors.

Shortly after reaching the sales arena, which is located on Pendleton's property, and finding a seat on the temporary bleachers I noted a very considerable disturbance going on at the entrance to the sales ring. People were pushing and jostling each other. The air was sizzling from the effects of a mode of profanity which, I understand, is the traditional prerogative of otherwise rather silent, restrained herdsmen.

The attention of some five hundred people was focused upon the scene. Suddenly there was a flash of color and a whirl of feathers. Henry P. Throckmorton, floating much in the fashion of a pheasant when preparing to light, sailed over the low gate and landed in the arena. He had followed me across the fields and was now searching me out.

The auctioneer, then engaged in selling lot number three, did not permit Throckmorton's entrance to interrupt the sale.

"Six seventy-five, six hundred and seventy-five dollars, six seventy-five, six seventy-five, six seventy-five, a fine individual, six seventy-five. I have six fifty bid. Who bids me six seventy-five? She is a third cousin to an international champion at Chicago. Six seventy-five. Who makes it six seventy-five? She is good foundation stock. Who bids me six seventy-five? You can't even raise 'em for that money, gentlemen. You are stealing this cow. I have six hundred and fifty dollars bid for the third cousin of a grand champion. You will be sorry if you lose her. Look her over. Look her over. Walk her around again. Let them all look at her. There is a quality head for you and what a depth to her. I have six hundred fifty bid for her. Who makes it six seventy-five? Look her over before it is too late."

Mr. Throckmorton, head on one side, was himself looking her over and undoubtedly recalling the pleasant afternoon he had spent a day or two before, breezing one of Mr. Bontecou's matrons and her calf around an orchard.

The attendant started leading the cow around the ring. She

showed him meager enthusiasm and stepped out slowly, bulling back on the halter shank.

This lackadaisical performance in no sense satisfied Throckmorton, so he lurched forward and assailed the third cousin of a grand champion from the rear.

There was a hoarse roar from the cow. She sprang forward, collided with the herdsman's hip and broke loose.

I had been vainly looking for my boy, Eddie Walsh, who always assists at these auctions. In spite of the general confusion I spotted him standing by the gate, raised my walking stick, attracted his attention and indicated that he was to remove Throckmorton.

Walsh, bedecked in the most flamboyant of his several black and white checked costumes, entered the ring. Without hesitation and in disregard of his sartorial finery, he took over the task of capturing Throckmorton, a task that no one would elect from choice.

The entire audience rose to their feet, cheered, laughed, clapped and called out advice, warnings and exhortations to Walsh.

Two ponderous jolly cattlemen from the distant state of Iowa, who were standing behind me, agreed that to enliven a sale by such a novel performance was a master stroke on the part of the auctioneer or the Dutchess County Committee.

One of the men, who had seen me wave my stick at Walsh, inquired if I was the auctioneer's partner.

When Walsh and Throckmorton had left the ring, amid great applause, both of them extremely disheveled, the sale continued. At some point in the fracas the bid of $675 which the auctioneer had so valiantly sought had apparently been obtained. He endeavored to procure $700, but failed and so knocked the cow down for $675.

Upon the arrival of the mail the next morning I received

a bill from the Dutchess County Aberdeen-Angus Breeders Association for $675 covering the price of lot number 3, a cow by Jacob's High Hope out of Smith Brothers' Sweet Lizzie, she out of Huntington's Winsome Pansy.

It is not my good fortune to enjoy a reputation for placidity, long suffering, meekness or tolerance. I do, however, make an effort to live without giving offense.

The receipt of this bill taxed my temper to the utmost and I at once wrote a cryptic note to Mr. Pendleton and sent it by hand, disclaiming the purchase of the cow. I assumed the incident closed. Not at all. Not at all.

Pendleton sent back a note by my own messenger reading, "You certainly had notice that the cow was being sold. You must have been conscious of the bid of $650 for it was often repeated. The auctioneer and many of us saw you raise your walking stick and register the bid of $675.

"As a matter of fact, the members of the Dutchess County Aberdeen-Angus Breeders Association present felt and expressed satisfaction that you had at last decided to join with us in the breeding of black cattle. We regretted, however, that you did not see fit to pay a little larger price and so acquire one of the better foundation cows from Briarcliff, Rally Farms, Schoonhoven, or Mrs. John Hanes's herd.

"The consignor of your new purchase lives in a distant part of the country and is not well known to us. He and his herdsman have returned home. The sale is over. The auctioneer is back again in the midwest. The event is past history. The consignor will of course expect you to pay for the cow. Payment is due immediately."

This entire event is so unpalatable to me that I exercise my prerogative of making no further comment other than to remark that whatever my feelings may have been in the past when Throckmorton crowed from the pine tree under my window at 3 A.M., they are now intensified.

In case anyone should be interested in such a trifle, I neglected to record that the name of my new cow is "Feltmuller's Gentle Jane."

Entirely unsolicited by me, Pendleton informs me that by the payment of $10.00 I may have the name changed, and suggests "Weatherford's Sweet Surprise," an attempt at humor as tepid as it is uncalled for.

Thus these little biographical notes which Dr. Sedgwick importuned me to pen, come to their close. Tomorrow at the White Elephant sale, Henry P. Throckmorton and I say "Hail and farewell" to each other.

A few moments ago I paused to take stock of my feelings respecting this separation, and it was borne in upon me that I and my household will feel a sense of loss as we revert to the quiet, uneventful, dignified pattern of former days, sans Throckmorton, but the die has been cast.

It is my fervent hope that Throckmorton may now move on to an environ which affords complete freedom for his prowess, full scope for his love of venturing against great odds, and that his gay, jubilant, swashbuckling temperament may never be subdued.

May I indulge in the prophecy that inasmuch as all things in nature are created to serve a useful purpose, so Throckmorton is so designed. He has it within him to make a distinguished contribution to someone's life, for truly his zest, courage and loyalty must influence those with whom he becomes associated.

In my present frame of mind, I find it hard to close these notes without recording a picture which I will ever retain of Throckmorton. It is of him standing on the edge of my terrace every late afternoon when I have been afield, standing bolt upright, waiting, waiting, waiting, no matter how long, for my return.

As the car approached the house, he met me on the wing.

When I opened the car door, he would pop in, stand up on the seat and in a torrent of clucks, tell me of the day's events.

It should be remembered that I am a bachelor, living without kith or kin. Such welcomes were not inconsequential to me.

I now make it clear in these notes and will make certain that my friend Mr. John Fitch, who has generously offered to conduct the White Elephant sale, will serve notice that I reserve the right, should I learn that Throckmorton is not happy and well cared for in his new home, to refund the purchase price, with interest to date if demanded, and reinstate him in my household.

John Fortescue Weatherford

Miss Pamela Patterson awoke assailed by the same depression and sense of futility which she had experienced for many mornings past.

On the first of these attacks she had immediately arisen in the belief that the cure lay in activity, but this only prolonged a day which was already far too long.

For some weeks she had concluded that isolation was at the root of her unhappiness, and that at her age one couldn't just muddle along, down through decades of time, friendless and being no part of the community in which one lived.

One had to have friendly, neighborly companionship, but one could not thrust one's self on a community.

She had come to Millbeck to make it her home, but a roof and four walls did not, in themselves, create a home.

When one's whole being is blanketed with depression, even breathing requires effort. Miss Patterson arose, slipped on a dressing gown and sat in front of the open casement window.

The air of the early September morning was wondrously clear and bracing. In the valleys a few of the swamp maples had donned their gay, going away colors.

To ponder and ponder is wearying, so her thoughts gradually wandered into lighter fields. She fell to wishing that she had been born into that make-believe world of long ago, where people had fairy godfathers to whom they turned in times of need. You just rubbed a lamp or something and the godparent appeared and you knew that all would be well.

Suddenly, while musing upon this world of fancy, the sound of a far off horn drifted in through the casement. "Young knights in armor," mused Miss Patterson, "sounded their horns as they approached their ladies' castles."

Once again the horn sounded, this time in a series of long, soft, mellow notes.

Her maid knocked, entered with the breakfast tray and said, "Excuse me, miss, but the cook told me that the Hunt is just to the North. She has heard Will Madden, the Huntsman, blowing his horn to call the little dogs to himself.

"The cook says that all the ladies and gentlemen will be going home now to have breakfast together and will sit a long time over their coffee, talking about how fine the hounds did, and how many big fences there were and how grand their own horses jumped 'em."

Pamela Patterson knew nothing about horses, hounds or fox hunting yet had long sensed that the Hunt was the focal point of the country community.

The Manager or head of the affair was a huge, gruff, auto-cratic old man, a Colonel something, who had been pointed out to her by one of the young ladies in the bank. She re-membered that the deposit slips on the table fluttered as he stumped out of the building.

Voices were now audible on the highway and the next moment horses' feet were crunching the gravel beneath her window.

An imperious voice rang out, "Let us respect this stretch of sward and the driveway. God bless me, it's the neatest bit of turf I've seen this side of Wimbleton. Those who are go-ing to hold horses, move them back towards the farm build-ings. And remember, we are out of the five cent zone so leave your coins with the butler. Look out! Look out, Dick Estey! Bless my soul, that colt will kick some one's new hat off."

Miss Patterson heard the bell ring, the door being opened and the same gruff voice saying, "Colonel Weatherford's re-spects to Miss Patterson. A number of us would like to use her telephone. Ah, what a gracious home has been made of this fine old place."

The speaker stumped to the telephone, "Good morning, Miss Margaret, Colonel Weatherford speaking. What do you hear from the hospital respecting your mother? Ah, that is capital news, capital. Commend me to her when you see her. Albert will bring you a bottle of port for her. Now then, the Kennels, please, and then my man Albert."

"Good morning, Mrs. Madden. The hound van is to take the road from Highminster to the old Van Heuten place, Miss Patterson's estate. Hounds will be on that road. Mrs. Mad-den, your husband never hunted the pack better than he did this morning. It must be the good care you take of him."

Silence, then, "Albert, twelve for breakfast and I would like Mr. and Mrs. Newcombe, Dr. Sedgwick, Madam Estey, and Mr. and Mrs. Edmonton for dinner if they are free. And

Albert, I want my entire staff to attend the White Elephant auction this afternoon to swell the attendance. Tell Walsh that he, not Clancy, is to be responsible for getting Throckmorton to the auction safely and controlling him during the sale. This is important."

The speaker thumped down the hall and out of the door.

A number of women used the telephone, arranging about breakfasts for various numbers of people, and for vans, grooms and cars to be sent.

Among those holding the horses or waiting their turn at the telephone, several bridge games were arranged.

Finally, the last of the riders disappeared down the driveway and the place was again shrouded in its customary silence.

Miss Patterson folded her arms on the window sill, inclined her head and rested it on her folded arms.

FROM ENID ASHLEY'S NOTE BOOK
Saturday (Morning)

What a cubbing morning this was—not cubbing really, but a gay, jubilant run on a perfect hunting morning. It was so lovely on these dear old hills of ours, with a rollicking breeze out of the N.W.

How hounds boiled along. Never, never did I see them turn and bend, shoulder to shoulder, on the line as they did today. Of all the stirring feats of hounds, none so rouses me as to see a pack, when running in full cry, bend to the line without falter.

The Colonel and Will Madden have the best young entry within my memory. They have great style and flash, think well of themselves and of each other, which counts for much, can explore a covert thoroughly in jig time and when they find and go away they carry such head, and cry to the line with such incredible clamor that you feel convinced they are going to run into their fox in the very next field. You live in continued excitement whenever they are running.

We put our fox to earth on the easterly slope of Robert Thatcher's farm after keeping him on his feet for an hour and ten minutes.

My precious, sensitive, sportloving little mare carried me so airily, and what monstrous fences and barways we had to navigate. They are a bit too high in that part of our country.

Dick Estey had the most horrible looking fall over a drop jump. He was riding his new Fair Play colt and should never have asked a colt to attempt such a fence. When Colonel Weatherford inquired if he was hurt, he said, "Oh no, sir, thank you, that was the easiest fall I've had today."

After the run we dropped in to telephone at the old Van Heuten place recently acquired and done over by a young person, Pamela Patterson. The pure artistry of the house and its embellishments are not to be matched in Millbeck. No one seems to have ever seen her. I have no doubt she considers us all very rowdy.

Stopped off at the Nortons'—scrambled eggs and sausages —worked my colt—took children to the dentist, then all hands for a quick dip in the club pool—perhaps the last this season—water cold but sun warm.

Saturday (Afternoon—Evening)

Lunched with the Newcombes, attended White Elephant sale—huge success—$1738.00 raised for fire truck—outstanding event was the purchase of Colonel Weatherford's famous rooster, Henry P. Throckmorton, by Pamela Patterson for $200. The entire assembly applauded and people were standing on tip toe to get a look at her. It was a generous, sporting and an exceedingly courageous thing for a young girl to have done. He is the most dreadful of birds.

The Colonel was so impressed with the purchase that he insisted on meeting Miss Patterson after the sale. He was very much taken with her, as well he might for she is both distinguished and engaging, but incredibly shy, sensitive and retiring.

Nothing would do but that she come to dinner. The old man sent his car for her, increased his dinner to twenty (I being included), and gave her the seat of honor.

Arthur Pendleton, whom she had finally out bid for Mr. Throckmorton, proposed her health in gracious words of welcome. She and Mr. Throckmorton were the talk of the table.

Before the evening was over she had joined the Hunt. Eddie Walsh was to teach her to ride, the Colonel was to find her a confidential horse and Dick Estey was taking her on at golf in the morning. She entered the Colonel's old Lancaster car with Eugene at the wheel, a gay and happy young person.

This was a day of many pleasant happenings and meetings for me.

Christmas Morning

Pamela Patterson awoke on Christmas morning conscious, decidedly conscious of a sense of well being. She reached her arm from beneath the gentle covering of time-softened linen sheets—sheets born amidst the gay smiles and laughter of Irish lassies, and rang for breakfast.

She then fell to contemplating upon her Christmas day. At ten by the clock she was to venture upon her first fox-hunt with Eddie Walsh as pilot. For this event she had practiced long, hard and faithfully.

How, she asked herself, could Eddie Walsh and all the others address themselves and their horses to the fences, even the low little ones which she had been jumping, with such indifference and composure.

At two o'clock she was to have Christmas dinner at Colonel Weatherford's with Mr. Pendleton and other gay and pleasant neighbors who in their friendliness had made her one of them.

At four o'clock she and Dick Estey and the George Ashleys were to head for the skiing hills of Vermont.

After thus reviewing the hours which lay ahead, she turned on the radio in search of Christmas tidings from England, where she had spent a number of happy Christmases.

From across the sea, the King was speaking to his people. "Her Majesty, the queen, joins with me in wishing all of you, in every part of the Empire, a Merry Christmas, and may God bless you, now and ever."

At Canterbury Cathedral the archbishop had reached the prayer of St. Chrysostom, one of the literary ornaments of our language. "Almighty God who has given us grace at this time with one accord to make our common supplications unto thee; and dost promise that when two or three are gathered together in Thy name, Thou wilt grant their request; fulfill now, O Lord, the desires and petitions of Thy servants as may be expedient for them; granting us in this world knowledge of Thy truth, and in the world to come, life ever lasting. Amen."

A famous actor who had brought pleasure to young and

old through the reading of Dickens' Christmas Carol, had ended his reading and was thanking all Londoners who had given towards making Christmas happy for the city's poor. He quoted:

> *"There passed a stranger yester eve*
> *For whom I set ere he did leave*
> *Food in the eating place*
> *Drink in the drinking place*
> *Sweet music in the listening place.*
> *He ate, he drank, he picked a rose.*
> *He rested where the clear burn flows.*
> *Then in the name of the sacred three*
> *Myself he blessed and my roof tree,*
> *My cattle and those dear to me.*
> *And then the lark said in her song,*
> *'Often and often from the skies,*
> *Goes the Christ in stranger guise.' "*

From a pine tree across the drive, a rooster crowed.

Pamela put her hands back of her head and lay a long time looking out of the window towards the tree. Finally she closed her eyes, put her hands over them, and murmured: " 'Often and often, from the skies, Goes the Christ in stranger guise.' On that dreary morning when I felt so lonesome and unhappy, I prayed, and asked for a fairy godfather. He came to me in stranger guise and brought me friends and happiness. I am grateful, very, very grateful.

"Merry Christmas, dear Mr. Throckmorton, Merry Christmas."

The four stories in this volume were originally privately printed. This edition was composed in Palatino types and printed at Heritage Printers, Inc., Charlotte, North Carolina. The binding was by A. Horowitz & Son, Clifton, New Jersey, and the slipcase by Brick & Ballerstein, Inc. Designed by Jean Callan King.

This edition is limited to fourteen hundred and fifty copies.